'No matter how ~~~~~~~~~~~~~~ ly engaged to be m~~~~~~~~~~~~~~ es to Emerald Tra~~~~~~~~~~~~~~ of a shock to Eme~~~~~~~~~~~~ into taking her into the Australian interior to find her fiancé, she never dreamed he would have the cunning to double-cross her. But now she knows what a ruthless, despicable sort of man Judah Renshaw really is, what will it take to persuade Emerald that marriage to him *won't* be a fate worse than death?

By the same author in Masquerade

COUNT ANTONOV'S HEIR
ZULU SUNSET
DIAMONDS IN THE DUST

TWENTY-SOVEREIGN BRIDE
CHRISTINA LAFFEATY

MILLS & BOON LIMITED
15–16 BROOK'S MEWS
LONDON W1A 1DR

All the characters in this book have no existence outside the imagination of the Author, and have no relation whatsoever to anyone bearing the same name or names. They are not even distantly inspired by any individual known or unknown to the Author, and all the incidents are pure invention.

The text of this publication or any part thereof may not be reproduced or transmitted in any form or by any means, electronic or mechanical, including photocopying, recording, storage in an information retrieval system, or otherwise, without the written permission of the publisher.

This book is sold subject to the condition that it shall not, by way of trade or otherwise, be lent, resold, hired out or otherwise circulated without the prior consent of the publisher in any form of binding or cover other than that in which it is published and without a similar condition including this condition being imposed on the subsequent purchaser.

First published in 1983 in serial form as
Bondswoman Bride *in*
My Weekly Magazine
*By D. C. Thomson Ltd.,
Dundee, Scotland.*

© Christina Laffeaty 1983, 1984

*This edition published 1984
by Mills & Boon Limited*

*Australian copyright 1984
Philippine copyright 1984*

ISBN 0 263 74930 4

*Set in 11 on 11½ pt Linotron Times
04–1284–58,000*

*Photoset by Rowland Phototypesetting Ltd
Bury St Edmunds, Suffolk
Made and printed in Great Britain by
Cox and Wyman Ltd, Reading*

CHAPTER ONE

EMERALD CLUNG to the railing of the steamship *Aurora*, the skirt of her gown moulded to her long slender thighs by the near gale-force winds, tendrils of dark-red hair escaping from the chignon in the nape of her neck and almost blinding her at times as the wind whipped them across her face. Immense rollers were tossing the vessel from side to side, and she knew that the members of the crew labouring on deck thought her mad not to keep to the shelter of her cabin as the other passengers were doing.

But the seemingly endless journey from England had proved her to be an excellent sailor, and she was far too excited, now that the undulating shoreline of New South Wales was in view, to miss a single moment of their arrival. The sun had just risen, bathing the scene in a brilliant rosy glow. To the north a bold and almost perpendicular cliff rose into the air; to the south loomed a wild, surf-beaten coast surmounted by sandstone headlands.

As Emerald fought to keep her footing she heard a muffled scream of terror coming from below. One of the poor wretched women travelling steerage, she thought with pity. When the ship prepared to enter the present troubled waters last night, the crew had battened the steerage passengers in like so much cargo. Seasick, frightened and overcrowded, it was only too easy to imagine the wretchedness of their claustrophobic condition. And they had so little to look forward to when the journey ended.

They were, Emerald had been told by one of the ship's officers, travelling to the new colony to hire themselves out as servants. It was their only escape from abject poverty or from the sweated labour of the slop-shops in England.

Emerald's mouth curved in a smile of joyful anticipation. How blessedly different her own journey's end was to be! For Andrew would be on the wharf to welcome her, to take her into his arms and claim her mouth with those tender kisses which she had yearned for with such intensity during their long separation . . .

With dramatic suddenness, the gale appeared to subside. Then she realised that the ship had entered an immense harbour, protected from the elements by its land-locked limits.

Emerald gazed with delight upon the seemingly unending wooded headlands with their curving bays which they were now passing.

'*Sydney Harbour*,' Andrew had written in one of his letters, '*has a beauty which almost defies description.*'

How right he had been, Emerald thought as she gazed at the windings and turnings of the inland sea. Each small bay or cove they passed delighted the eye, and each verdant island seemed like an emerald set in the shimmering silver of the surrounding water.

Now the vessel was steering towards a wharf cut in the living rock. Other passengers were cautiously venturing on deck. Emerald tore herself away from the railing and went below to tidy her hair and bring her luggage on deck.

All her worldly possessions had easily been packed into two carpet-bags. She was wearing a gown of rose-coloured fine worsted, its simple bodice cut modestly high to the throat, its skirt falling in ample folds to her feet. It was the same colour as her best gown, which, she had worn, over a year ago, on the night of the Standish ball. With the two younger Standish children she had crouched at the top of the stairs, watching the dancing below. And Andrew, the second of her employers' two grown-up sons, had spied them there, and had brought up some sweetmeats for them, and after his two young sisters had been put to bed he had waltzed with Emerald in the darkened corridor to the music from the ballroom below, and kissed her for the first time . . .

She smiled, and then sighed as other, less pleasant, memories came crowding back. Their idyllic romance had lasted precisely a month before it was discovered by Mrs Standish. The repercussions had been swift and inexorable. Emerald had broken the unwritten law that a governess should not become romantically involved with a member of her employers' family. She had been dismissed immediately without a reference. And to make doubly sure that the love affair would die, Mr Standish had packed his younger son off into the navy . . .

Emerald picked up her carpet-bags and went on deck, shrugging off the memory of the miserable months which had followed. Months during which she had found it impossible to obtain another situation because of the damning lack of a reference from the Standishes. Months of wretched loneliness, wondering where Andrew was, or whether they would ever meet again . . .

On deck, everyone was now jostling excitedly in anticipation of disembarking. Emerald's eager gaze scanned the crowded wharf below for a glimpse of Andrew, but in that turbulent sea of humanity it was impossible to pick him out.

The first-class passengers were being allowed to disembark first. They were being met by liveried coachmen or by finely-dressed friends and relations. As she waited for her own turn to go ashore, Emerald again spared a thought of pity for the women in steerage. Having had to endure the worst of conditions on board, they would be the very last to be allowed to disembark.

The crowd on the wharf had cleared somewhat by the time she found herself standing on firm soil for the first time in weeks. The morning sun beat savagely down on her head and she narrowed her eyes against its glare as she searched for Andrew. Perhaps he had changed in the intervening months, had grown a beard and whiskers . . .

She smiled a little as she tried to imagine what he looked like, now that he was no longer either an English gentleman or a naval officer but a farmer in the interior of New South Wales. Andrew had defied his father by buying himself out of the navy as soon as his ship docked in Sydney Harbour. He had acquired a free grant of land, and had begun to write Emerald long, ardent, but unavoidably infrequent letters, hampered by the distance between them. But his love for her had been expressed in undiminished terms in each of those letters. He was saving as hard as he was able so that he could send her the fare to New South Wales, and then they would be married.

She herself had been unable to save a farthing. With both her parents dead and having no close relatives, she had been forced to seek refuge with the woman who had been her childhood Nanny. Emerald had never lost touch with her, and once, during their brief illicit romance, she had taken Andrew to meet Nanny in her furnished rooms in Islington. And it was to Nanny's address that he had written to Emerald once he arrived in New South Wales. By giving private tuition to a handful of pupils, Emerald had earned barely enough to pay Nanny for her keep, and had sunk steadily into debt.

And then the miracle had happened which had made it possible for her to come and join Andrew . . .

The thought snapped off abruptly in her mind. Other than sailors and dock-workers and a uniformed dragoon with mutton-chop whiskers who was patrolling the wharf, there were few civilians about now, and the steerage passengers were beginning to disembark.

Where was Andrew?

Emerald chewed at her lower lip. She had written hastily, telling him about the death of a distant cousin whose existence Emerald had almost forgotten. The cousin had left her fifty guineas in her will, and as soon as Emerald learnt of the bequest she had penned a letter to Andrew, telling him that she planned to sail for Sydney on the *Aurora*. That letter should have arrived in Sydney more than twelve weeks ago.

She became aware that a group of sailors were

subjecting her to lecherous leers, and she turned a freezing glance on them. But she was glad when the dragoon with the mutton-chop whiskers approached her, and asked politely, 'Can I be of any assistance, miss?'

The dragoons, Andrew had told her in one of his letters, did dual service as militia and policemen, and the wharf was obviously this one's regular responsibility, for the sailors appeared to know him.

'Well . . .' Emerald hesitated. It would be foolish to fly into a panic at this stage and ask for official investigation into Andrew's failure to arrive. He had to travel a long distance from the interior and *anything*—some slight mishap like the sudden lameness of a bullock—could have delayed him.

'No, thank you,' she amended. 'I am to be met quite soon.'

'I see. All the same, miss, I think I'll stay close just in case those jack-tars—' he jerked a thumb in the direction of the sailors '—should try to overstep the mark.'

She thanked him with a subdued smile. Nothing had prepared her for the intense heat, and apart from her anxiety about Andrew she was becoming acutely and uncomfortably aware that her clothes were totally unsuited to the climate of New South Wales.

Then, with a rush of relief, she saw that a new crowd of men were approaching the wharf. Judging by the dustiness of their boots, by their sunburnt faces and their workmanlike clothing, they were not natives of Sydney but had come in from the interior. Andrew would be sure to be among them.

The dragoon appeared to know most of the

newcomers by name, and she listened mechanically as he exchanged news and gossip with them, her eyes all the while scanning the new arrivals for a glimpse of Andrew.

'How are things up your way, Matt?' she heard the dragoon ask one of the men.

'Rough,' was the gloomy reply. 'The Murrumbidgee's in flood again and some of the tracks are impassable. Many folk will be cut off for weeks.'

'That's too bad.'

'Yeah, well . . .' The man shrugged, and walked on. He, and all the others following him, cast curious, appreciative glances at Emerald as they passed. None of them was Andrew.

Her nails were digging into the palms of her hands with growing tension. As the surge of newcomers diminished to an occasional trickle, she picked up her carpet-bags and approached the dragoon.

'I—the gentleman who was to meet me—Well, I heard someone talk about flooding and impassable tracks, and I wondered . . .'

'Who are you waiting for, miss? Perhaps I know him.'

'His name is Andrew Standish. Originally he took up a grant of land at a place called Wallalong, but now he farms at Coorabee Creek . . .'

'Yes, I know him slightly,' the dragoon interrupted. 'He won't be coming in to Sydney this trip.'

Emerald stared at him in dismay. 'How can you be sure? Andrew was expecting me! Are the roads between Sydney and Coorabee Creek impassable?'

The dragoon shook his head. 'No, miss, there's nothing wrong with the roads. I saw Judah Renshaw a little while ago. He's from Coorabee, and that's how I know that Mr Standish won't be coming in, because Jude picked up the mail for everyone at Coorabee, and he would have left Mr Standish's mail if he was coming in as well.'

Emerald clenched her hands tightly together. 'Then Andrew must be ill! That's the only possible explanation! Do you know where I could find this Mr Renshaw? He'll have news of Andrew, and at least he could take me with him to Coorabee Creek when he leaves Sydney.'

An odd look crossed the dragoon's face. 'Yes, I *could* take you to meet Jude, miss. The trouble is—well, there's bad blood between him and Mr Standish. Real bad blood. Jude wouldn't do a favour for any friend or relation of Mr Standish.'

An angry flush stained Emerald's cheeks. 'Oh, wouldn't he? What could he possibly have against Andrew?'

'I don't know the ins and outs of it,' the dragoon said, but it was very clear from his expression that he *did* know, but was not prepared to tell. 'I only know that the two of them came to blows a while back, and that if a couple of stockmen had not forcibly dragged Jude away he would have killed young Mr Standish with his bare hands.'

Emerald's blue eyes flashed fire at the thought of Andrew being assaulted by the unknown but obviously brutish, murderous Judah Renshaw. 'Was he seriously hurt?' she demanded. 'Could *that* be why he was unable to meet the *Aurora* today?'

'No, no! It happened several months ago, and Mr Standish has quite recovered. I can't imagine why he did not come to meet you, miss, but . . .' The dragoon hesitated. 'If you were to ask Jude to take you to him, he would refuse. And if he *did* agree, then I'm afraid it might be only so that—well, so that he could wreak further vengeance on Mr Standish by subjecting you to humiliation, perhaps, because it is very clear that there is a personal relationship between you and his enemy.'

How on earth, Emerald wondered, could gentle, sensitive Andrew have made such an implacable foe? She could only imagine that Judah Renshaw was the kind of loutish backwoodsman who could not stomach someone of breeding and refinement and superior intelligence, like Andrew, and that his hatred was based on blind prejudice.

'Your best course,' she heard the dragoon go on, 'would be to hire a conveyance and an experienced driver who is handy with a gun to take you to Coorabee. I know someone I could recommend . . .'

'No,' Emerald interrupted in a voice which was taut with anger and anxiety and the beginning of despair. 'I could not afford that. Is there no one else here from Coorabee who might take me?'

The dragoon shook his head. 'Jude picked up all the mail. That means he is the only one from the district meeting the *Aurora*.'

'If he hates Andrew so much,' Emerald asked with a frown, 'why does he trouble to pick up and deliver his mail?'

Once again she received the impression that the dragoon knew more than he was prepared to say, even though his explanation was quite plausible. 'He doesn't deliver it in person. Whoever comes in from Coorabee collects the mail and leaves it in the general store out there to be picked up.'

Emerald thought hard for a moment. Her fifty-guinea bequest had paid her debts in London and her fare to New South Wales, and she was practically destitute. Andrew had either failed to receive her letter, or else he was ill. She *had* to reach Coorabee Creek, and Judah Renshaw represented her only chance of doing so. Much as it would go against the grain, she would have to deny her love for Andrew, deny that she even knew him, and use all her guile to persuade Renshaw to take her with him into the interior.

She looked up at the dragoon. 'Please, just introduce me to this Judah Renshaw, and don't say anything about my connection with Andrew Standish. My name is Miss Emerald Travers. I'll handle the situation from there.'

The dragoon's eyes softened under her appealing gaze. 'Very well, Miss Travers. Jude is a hard man to fool, but—I wish you luck.'

He led the way along the wharf to where a man was supervising the unloading of stores from a small vessel. 'Jude, there's a lady here who wishes to meet you,' the dragoon called.

The man turned. Emerald's first surprise was that he was not the red-faced, bovine lout of her imagination. 'Miss Emerald Travers—Mr Judah Renshaw,' the dragoon introduced them, and moved discreetly away.

Judah Renshaw was perhaps thirty, tall and lithe and with more than a suggestion of strength about him. She looked at his hard-muscled arms, and when he held out his hand to her she thought of it attempting to throttle the life out of Andrew. She shook hands with him, trying to hide her hostility.

'How do you do, Miss Travers,' he said, studying her.

She appraised him in turn. His hair was the

colour of silver-gilt, no doubt bleached that way by the sun, and contrasted strongly with the mahogany tan of his clean-shaven face. His features were even, his eyes an unusual tawny shade flecked with green and set between dark lashes. He would have been quite dramatically handsome were it not for the grim, hard-bitten lines about his mouth and the cynical expression in his eyes.

'What can I do for you?' One heavy, dark-blond eyebrow was raised at her.

Emerald was at pains to make her voice even and businesslike. 'I understand that you know a Mr Andrew Standish.'

His eyes hardened. 'To my misfortune, yes.'

She gritted her teeth. 'Do you happen to know if he is ill?'

'I wish I could have replied that he was,' Judah Renshaw returned with chill malevolence. 'Unfortunately, as far as I know, he is in rude health. Why? What are you to him?'

Emerald pretended to shade her eyes against the sun so that they would not betray her. 'Nothing. I have never met him.' She burnt to ask what possible harm Andrew could ever have done this man, but sensed that he would tell her to mind her own business. Besides, it would only arouse his suspicions if she showed too much interest in his feud with Andrew.

Before she could go on, Renshaw consulted his pocket-watch, and said, 'I have some other business to attend to now. If you would care to walk a little distance with me, you could tell me what your interest is in Standish.'

Without waiting for her consent he picked up Emerald's carpet-bags, and she fell into step beside him. She was aware that he was studying her with a sidelong, frank glance of appraisal which would have angered her even if she had not already been hostile towards him.

They were walking towards a structure made of wood, and Emerald saw that it had no roof but appeared to be something in the nature of a stockade. Crowds of men, obviously come in from the interior, were gathered outside, and as Emerald approached with Judah Renshaw she realised that girls who had travelled steerage on the *Aurora* were being herded into it by a formidable-looking older woman. The situation slotted into place in Emerald's mind.

The girls were putting themselves up for hire, and the men had come to acquire servants to take back to their wives in the interior.

Her attention and her sympathies were still centred upon the girls entering the stockade when she heard Judah Renshaw say, 'Well, if you have never met Andrew Standish, why are you asking questions about him?'

'I left England,' Emerald began the story she had decided upon, 'for personal reasons, to make a new life out here. Through mutual acquaintances, Mr Standish's parents heard that I was to make the journey, and they asked me to deliver a package to him which they did not wish to entrust to the mail. He was to have met me at the harbour, and in return for delivering the package safely, help me to establish myself in New South Wales.'

'I see. Well, I'm afraid I can't throw any light on the matter. I do know that he had no plans to come to Sydney. If you would like to write him a note I'll ensure that he gets it, and you could find lodgings and wait. Assuming that he *wants* the package, you should not have to wait longer than three weeks . . .'

'You are neighbours?' Emerald interrupted, ignoring his advice.

The grim lines about Judah Renshaw's mouth deepened. 'In a manner of speaking, yes.'

'Then—could you possibly take me with you when you return?'

'I'm afraid not. My dray will be fully loaded, and I shall have room for only one passenger.' He glanced towards the entrance of the stockade, where the older woman in charge of the girls was allowing the men to file inside. Then his glance returned briefly to Emerald. 'Now, if you will excuse me . . .'

'Wait!' she said desperately. 'I know what is going on in there. You are about to pick one of the girls?'

'Yes. I have been told there are a few who might be suitable.'

She took a deep breath. 'Would—would you consider *me* suitable?'

He whistled through his teeth, and gave her a long, thoughtful stare. 'You really *are* anxious to deliver that package to Standish, aren't you? Its contents must be pretty valuable for you to go to such lengths!'

She had not missed the taunting suspicion in his voice. With assumed candour, she said, 'It isn't that. As far as the package is concerned, I merely wish to be rid of responsibility for the wretched thing. But because I had been promised compensation by Mr Standish and valuable introductions which would have enabled me to start a new life in the colony, I foolishly spent the little money I had ear-marked to tide me over upon my arrival. So now I am penniless, stranded and quite desperate. I could not pay for lodgings for three nights, let alone three weeks.'

'I see,' Judah said thoughtfully. He studied her for a long moment. 'I don't suppose you know anything about looking after children?'

'Oh, but indeed I do! For the past six years, since my parents died of cholera when I was eighteen, I have been earning my living as a governess. My father was a clergyman, you see, and left no money.'

'It is beginning to sound as if you would do admirably, Miss Travers! Tell me—what were the personal reasons which prompted you to seek a new life in the colony?'

'A broken romance,' she answered expressionlessly.

'Well, you are obviously honest and trustworthy,' he observed, 'or the Standishes would not have asked you to deliver a valuable package to their son. For the rest—my instinct tells me that you are precisely what we have been looking for.'

He smiled for the first time, and it was quite amazing how it softened and altered his face, so that Emerald felt a stirring of guilt.

'I'll tell you all about the children later. In the meantime, you had better have this.' He pulled a draw-string bag of soft hide from his pocket. 'There are twenty sovereigns in there. It is the commission I would have had to pay the female dragon in charge of the girls if I had chosen one of your calibre, so I consider it fair that you should have it instead.'

Emerald was staring at the bag of money, uncertain what to do. She had not counted on this unexpected development. Before she could decide how to react, Judah reached for the reticule on her arm and dropped the draw-string bag inside it. Then he picked up her carpet-bags and led the way briskly to where a row of hackney cabs were waiting for customers. He opened the door of one of the cabs, and handed her inside.

'Use the money to buy yourself some light-weight clothes. You will need them in the interior.' He closed the door, and Emerald heard him address the cabbie. 'Take the lady to O'Connors'. Wait for her while she shops, and deliver her at the George Hotel no later than one-thirty.'

With a feeling of panic, Emerald sank back in her seat. She had meant merely to trick Judah Renshaw into taking her with him. Once she was at Coorabee Creek, she would have told him that she had no intention of being governess to his children, and she had no doubt at all that his wife would prove to be an ally. The last thing a woman married to someone like Judah Renshaw would want was an attractive governess sharing the confinement of their isolated lives in the interior. Renshaw would have had to bow to the galling knowledge that he had been tricked into helping his enemy, and it would have been no more than he deserved after his brutal assault on Andrew.

But the money complicated the whole matter. She couldn't possibly accept it or spend it.

And yet, if she did not spend the money, Judah Renshaw would want to know her reasons. He would worm the truth out of her, and abandon her in Sydney.

She reached inside her reticule for the money, as if it would somehow present her with a solution to the problem. Instead, her fingers encountered the bundle of Andrew's letters which she carried with her.

Why had he not met the *Aurora* today? Renshaw had said that he was not ill . . . A possible explanation suddenly struck her. Twelve or thirteen weeks ago, when her letter would have arrived in Sydney, it might well have been Judah Renshaw who picked up the mail for Coorabee. His rage against Andrew could still have been raw and new enough to prompt him to a malicious destruction of anything addressed to Andrew, so that the latter was totally unaware that Emerald would be arriving in Sydney. Yes, that had to be the explanation.

As she had so often done before in times of anxiety, Emerald began to re-read Andrew's letters for comfort, choosing one of the earlier ones first. It began,

> There are not words enough to tell you how much I miss you and long for you. I try to comfort myself in my unbearable loneliness by counting the money I have so far saved towards paying your passage to New South Wales, but it remains so pitifully inadequate, my darling. I want you so desperately by my side. Oh, dearest, how am I to endure the long, long separation before I can at last make you my own?

Moist-eyed, she turned to another of the letters. This was the last she had received from him before she sailed for New South Wales.

My darling, in answer to your anxious question, I have now saved the princely sum of fifteen sovereigns towards your fare. That would be sufficient to pay for a steerage ticket, but I shudder at the thought of your having to make that long voyage under such wretched conditions. Besides, my dearest one, it is not only a matter of paying for your passage alone. There is so much else you would need. Believe me, you would not survive for a week in what passes in England for a lady's summer wear. It is absolutely essential that I should have sufficient funds saved to pay for a basic wardrobe for you, suitable in this killing heat . . .'

Emerald stopped reading, and stared pensively before her. At the time, she had dismissed his comments about a wardrobe with impatience, and had gone on to read his assurances of love and longing. She had been about to write back, telling him that she would somehow make do with the clothes she possessed, and that she was more than willing to travel steerage. But then the bequest of fifty guineas from her distant cousin had changed everything.

Now, Emerald had to confess that Andrew had been perfectly right about the need for a suitable wardrobe. Judah Renshaw had also said as much, which must mean that it was even hotter inland than it was in Sydney. And the things she would need were no doubt obtainable only in the town . . .

'This here is O'Connors', miss,' the cabbie's voice broke into her thoughts. 'The best store in Sydney.'

She allowed him to help her from the cab, and turned resolutely towards the store. Andrew had already saved fifteen sovereigns at the time he last wrote to her; she would spend that amount, and he would repay Judah Renshaw.

After Emerald had purchased four light-weight gowns, it became obvious that she would need other accoutrements too. Almost nothing she possessed would be suitable in the interior, the assistant assured her earnestly.

By the time the cabbie was driving Emerald to the George Hotel for her meeting with Judah Renshaw, there was little left over from the twenty sovereigns he had given her. Fatalistically, she decided that she and Andrew would just have to scrimp and scrape in order to repay Renshaw the full amount owing to him.

She had changed out of her worsted gown with relief, and was wearing one of her new purchases, a gown of green lawn with a low-cut neckline trimmed with lace. A light straw bonnet of a deeper shade of green decorated with flowing ribbons, framed her face and provided a perfect foil for her red hair.

Judah Renshaw was waiting outside the door of the George Hotel. He gave her a look of appraising approval as he helped her from the cab, and to her deep annoyance Emerald found herself blushing under his scrutiny.

He paid off the driver, and commanded a hotel flunkey to take Emerald's boxes and packages and load them on to his dray in the hotel's coach-yard. Then, with his hand lightly upon her elbow, he steered her towards the door of the hotel.

'We shall have luncheon in civilised luxury before we start the journey to Coorabee. I have engaged a private room.'

A conflicting mixture of guilt and defiance warred within Emerald. She had already spent his money; she did not wish to be further in his debt by eating food expensively provided by him.

On the other hand, he was a brutish bully who had almost killed Andrew—dear, gentle Andrew who could not conceivably have done anything to deserve such violence. And Renshaw was so vindictive still that he would refuse to help anyone connected with Andrew. Furthermore, it was almost certainly due to him that Emerald's letter had not reached Andrew. It was entirely Renshaw's fault that she had been forced to deceive him.

'Here we are,' she heard him say as a uniformed page bowed them into a room where a table had been laid for two, and conveyed an unmistakably festive air. Champagne was cooling in an ice-bucket and the table had been decorated with a bowl of exotic flowers.

Judah Renshaw's voice held a slightly sardonic note. 'I thought you would appreciate the illusion of a romantic celebration. After all, no matter how it came about, we are undoubtedly engaged to be married . . .'

'*What!*' Emerald spun around and stared at him. With slowly mounting shock and disbelief she saw that he was entirely serious. 'I—there has been a mistake. I hired myself out to you as a *governess* . . .'

'My dear girl.' His eyebrows had risen. 'If there has been a mistake, then it was on your part alone, and a very foolish one at that.'

'But—I was told—those girls in the stockade . . .

They had travelled steerage on the *Aurora*. I was reliably informed that they were to hire themselves out as servants . . .'

'Your informant was not as reliable as you imagined. Most of those girls *do* start the journey with the intention of hiring themselves out as servants. But it's an open secret that a female agent arranges to travel on the same ship, and recruits as many as possible of the suitable ones to be chosen instead as wives for men from the interior. Those remaining would have made their own way to the marketplace to hire themselves out.'

He gave Emerald a cynical smile. 'Ignorant though you may have been, you could not seriously have believed, surely, that I would have paid twenty sovereigns for a *governess*?'

'*Paid* . . .' Emerald's voice cracked as she took in the humiliating implications of the word.

'Yes, indeed. And since you have spent the money which I laid out on purchasing you, you have no alternative but to make the best of things.'

'*I'd sooner die!*'

'Indeed?' He reached for her before she could evade him, jerking her towards him. She could tell by the glitter of his eyes that her violent reaction had bruised his pride. 'Then I shall have to convince you that marriage to me *won't* be a fate worse than death!'

One arm imprisoned her while his free hand traced the shape of her body, and at the same time his mouth invaded hers with a practised sensuality which she recognised even as she responded to it.

Passion, primitive and wholly demoralising and never before experienced with such intensity, thundered through Emerald. When he let her go, looking down at her with a triumphant half-smile, shame and self-disgust washed over her. She wanted to do something violent to him to relieve her own feelings; she longed to claw at his face, to etch a trail of bloody scratches around that satanic smiling mouth.

But she was no match for him physically, and so she tried to flail him with words instead. 'You have merely convinced me that you are utterly beneath contempt! What kind of pathetic and inadequate man would need to resort to *buying* himself a wife?'

Even as she uttered the words, Emerald knew that they had been a foolish choice. Judah Renshaw might be many things; pathetic and inadequate were not among them. He shrugged the insult aside, and said with brutal candour,

'I have never had to pay for a woman, if that is what you are trying to imply, and I shall have no need to do so in the future if you should insist on keeping our marriage on a platonic plane. Undeniable though your physical charms are, Miss Emerald Travers, they are not what I have paid twenty sovereigns for.'

He paused to uncork the champagne and poured out two glasses. Looking at her over the rim of his own glass, he continued, 'My sister and her husband were recently killed, and it was left to me to bring up their two children. I cannot do so without a wife. Whatever your past might be, I summed you up as a woman of refinement and education, and I sensed that you had compassion because of the way you watched those seasick, wretched girls entering the stockade. Those are the qualities for which I shall be marrying you, whether you like it or not.'

'Surely a governess would have answered the case?' she demanded incredulously. 'There is no need for something as drastic as marriage . . .'

'Indeed there is,' he cut in with a grim smile. 'If you had been in your fifties, shaped like a haystack and with a face to match, I would have employed you as governess to my niece and my nephew. But no one looking at you would believe for a moment that you are not my mistress.'

'I am surprised,' Emerald said scathingly, 'that you should jib at the thought of being said to keep a mistress!'

'Personally, I don't care a snap of my fingers for what people might say of me. But because I have no intention of having the children hurt by any slurs cast upon the character of the woman who is to have the care of them, you must be married to me. Moreover, so that no one will be in any doubt that we *are* legally and respectably married, the ceremony will be performed in the courthouse at Coorabee Creek.'

'No, it won't! Even *you* could not hope to force me—'

'Indeed I couldn't,' he agreed calmly. 'But I have twenty sovereigns invested in you, and I *could* use the law to ensure that I am compensated. Repay me, and we'll call it quits.' He gave her a calculating look. 'You have in your possession a package intended for Andrew Standish, which must clearly contain valuables. You have discharged your obligations to his parents, and his failure to meet your ship absolves you from further responsibility. So hand the package over to me, and I shall consider myself fairly compensated.'

'*You* . . .' Emerald began with furious indignation, and then stopped as she was suddenly struck by the absurdity of this whole argument.

She had never had any intention, in the first place, of being governess to what she had believed to be his children. The fact that he had sought to acquire a wife instead did not alter anything. Anger had almost caused her to lose sight of her true objective—to reach Coorabee Creek, and Andrew. Once safely there, she would refuse to marry Judah just as she had intended to refuse the post of governess, and Andrew would repay his wretched twenty sovereigns.

'Well?' Judah demanded, watching her. 'Will you hand over Standish's package in exchange for your freedom?'

'No,' Emerald said sullenly. 'I'll go with you to Coorabee Creek.'

He nodded with satisfaction, a triumphant smile curving his mouth. 'I was merely testing your reaction, never doubting for a moment what it would be. I knew that my judgment of you was not at fault. You undertook to deliver the package to Standish, and nothing would make you go back on your bond. You possess both honour and integrity.'

He took her chin in his hand, tilting up her face. 'You will suit me very well indeed, Emerald Travers,' he said softly. 'And once I have made you forget that broken romance of yours, you will find that I suit you equally well. I would not be holding you to our agreement if I did not feel sure of that.'

He drew his index finger lightly over her lips, and let her go. He had already inspired in her helpless rage, guilt, primitive desire and self-disgust, and now she was aware of totally new emotions.

She was gripped by fear of what he would do

when he found out how thoroughly she had duped him. But even stronger than her fear was an overwhelming sense of shame. She felt shabby and squalid because of what she had been forced to do. All her defiance and sense of righteousness had evaporated, and she knew that she could not continue the deceit for a moment longer.

Without looking at him, she said, 'There—was no broken romance. Everything I told you was a lie. I'm desperate to reach Coorabee Creek because I've been betrothed to Andrew Standish for the past year, and I have come to marry him. I knew, from what the dragoon said, that you would not help me if I told you the truth. So—I set out to use you . . .'

He said nothing. The silence between them stretched ominously, and at last she forced herself to meet his eyes. They held rage and disillusionment, and as their glances locked she could read his growing and implacable resolve to make her pay for having played him for such a fool.

She flinched, and took a step backwards. 'Did you think I was going to strike you?' he asked icily. 'I don't hit women.'

She licked her dry lips. 'But—you mean to punish me. I can only appeal to you not to leave me stranded and penniless in Sydney . . .'

'Have no fear,' he interrupted with cold deliberation. 'That would not be punishment enough. You deserve something far worse, and I'm going to savour every moment of my revenge, Miss Emerald Travers!'

She stammered, 'What . . . what are you going to do?'

'I'm going to take you to Andrew Standish.' He

gave an ugly laugh, and added with menace, 'Believe me, you will be wishing with all your heart that I had left you to starve in Sydney instead!'

CHAPTER TWO

JUDAH RENSHAW pulled at the bell-cord. As if they had been hovering outside the door, serving-maids entered with covered silver dishes and set them on the table.

With exaggerated courtesy, Judah drew out a chair for Emerald, so that she was forced to sit down. She stared at the food on her plate, her normally healthy appetite having utterly deserted her.

His implicit threat could mean only one thing. The trip to the interior would take three or four days and nights, during which time she would be alone with him and at his mercy.

'*If he did agree to take you,*' the dragoon had said, '*I'm afraid it might be only so that he could wreak further vengeance on Mr Standish by humiliating you.*'

And now she had given him a stronger and more personal reason for exacting revenge. It had been a disastrous mistake to blurt out the truth like that. Everything she already knew about him should have warned her against it. If only he hadn't shamed her by telling her that she possessed honour and integrity, and accepted her lies so unquestioningly . . .

But it was profitless to waste time in regrets. As

soon as the serving-maids withdrew from the room, she stopped pretending to toy with her food, and looked up at Judah.

'I've changed my mind. I don't wish to go to Coorabee Creek with you.'

'That's too bad,' he interrupted crisply. '*I* haven't changed *mine*.'

'You can't take me with you by force . . .'

'*No?* Would you care to put it to the test?'

She tried to hide her growing fear. 'Any other man,' she said scathingly, 'would want to wash his hands of me in the circumstances. If it's a question of your twenty sovereigns . . .'

'It isn't. And I am not "*any other man*".' He showed his teeth in a ferocious grin. 'You lied and schemed and made a fool of me in order to reach your fiancé at Coorabee Creek. Do you think I would allow myself to be cheated of my revenge?'

Emerald pushed back her chair and stood up. 'I'm going to walk out of here now. If you try to stop me I'll make such a scene that you won't be able to show your face in Sydney again . . .'

He was on his feet too, moving towards her with grim, unhurried determination. She let out a piercing scream.

It was cut off almost at once as he pulled her into his arms and covered her mouth with his own. She tried to fight him, but his arms were like steel bands enclosing her and, more insidiously still, she found her senses responding treacherously to what was no more than a physical assault, a means of silencing her. She heard the door opening as one of the hotel staff, who had heard her scream, came to investigate.

Judah lifted his mouth from hers, but held her

firmly pressed to him, her face buried against his chest so that she could scarcely breathe, let alone utter a sound.

'My bride-to-be thought she had seen a mouse,' she heard him explain smoothly. 'She will have to grow accustomed to far more fearsome creatures in the colony, will she not?'

'Yes, indeed, Mr Renshaw, sir.'

When the door had been discreetly closed upon them again, Judah relaxed his grip on Emerald's body. Instead, his hands moved to encircle her throat.

'I know precisely how and where to apply just sufficient pressure to render you unconscious,' he said with ominous calm. 'And I'll do it if you show the slightest sign of making a scene. I'll simply pull you into my arms and pretend to kiss you, as any hot-blooded lover would do, and you will appear to have fainted under the force of our mutual passion. So the choice is yours—either you board my dray with dignity, of your own volition, or I'll dump your senseless body on it like a sack of potatoes.'

She had not the slightest doubt that he would do what he threatened. Moreover, all the cards were stacked in his favour. He was known and respected at this hotel, and everyone was aware that he had ordered a special luncheon to celebrate his engagement. She had been seen entering the place with him of her own free will, so who would now believe that she was being held under duress?

No, it would be useless even to try and make a secret appeal for help to any of the hotel staff . . .

'Now sit down,' Judah's voice broke through her desperate thoughts, 'and enjoy your celebration meal.'

He returned to his own seat, and refilled their glasses with champagne. He lifted his, and said mockingly, 'To our journey into the interior!'

Emerald glared at him, and forced herself to swallow some of the excellent food. She would need it, for there was no knowing when she would next be able to eat. She had every intention of escaping from Judah Renshaw before they had left Sydney.

Her thoughts were racing. If she could contrive to sit in the back of his dray, she ought to be able to throw her carpet-bags from the vehicle at a moment when his attention was occupied with driving through traffic, and scramble off in their wake. By the time he became aware of her absence she would, with luck, have lost herself in a crowd.

What had previously seemed an unthinkable fate—being stranded in Sydney—was now to be strived for at all costs. She would return to the harbour and ask the friendly dragoon with the mutton-chop whiskers to help her to obtain temporary employment—no matter how menial—and then bide her time until someone else from Coorabee Creek visited Sydney so that she could request his escort into the interior.

But almost as though he had read her mind, Judah frustrated Emerald's entire plan from the outset. He had settled the account at the hotel, and with his hand firmly on her arm, guided her to where his dray was waiting.

'There's room enough for you on the driving seat,' he said.

'I would prefer to put as great a physical distance as possible between us,' she responded coldly. 'I'll sit in the back. I'm sure a space could be made for me among the stores and provisions . . .'

'You'll sit with me,' he cut in, his eyes glinting at her in perfect understanding. 'Come, I'll help you up.'

Sullenly, with mounting despair, she was forced to submit. He cracked a long-handled whip over the heads of the span of bullocks and the dray began to trundle its cumbersome way through the streets of Sydney.

The signs of civilisation were all too soon behind them, and ahead stretched only the hot, red, dusty hills out of Sydney towards the interior.

Emerald's spirits suddenly rose when she saw a small crowd of men milling about in the distance, and then became aware that the dray was approaching an impressive turnpike gate. That meant that Judah would have to stop to pay a toll, and it also meant that the gate would be manned by a person of some authority.

As they drew nearer, the crowd of men mobbed the dray, and began to urge Judah to hire them.

'Mr Renshaw, sir, I'll work for five shillings a week—'

'*I'm* willin' to hire for a twelve-month—'

'If you'll have *me*, Mr Renshaw, I'll take work by the piece—'

'Sorry, fellows,' Judah silenced them. 'I already have all the hands I need.' He added with a grin, 'Spent all your money in Sydney on booze?'

The men laughed sheepishly, acknowledging the truth of his taunt, and fell into step beside the dray as it headed towards the turnpike. Their mood was philosophical. There would be other vehicles making for the interior, other chances of being hired.

Emerald sat tensely on the edge of the seat. She, too, would take her chance by waiting at the turnpike after the keeper had rescued her from Judah.

At a bellowed command the bullocks shambled to a halt, and Judah handed the required toll to the turnpike-keeper. The latter was a middle-aged man with a weatherbeaten face and grizzled hair.

His jaw dropped as Emerald launched into her desperate appeal. 'Please—I know you must have a certain authority vested in you. This man is abducting me, taking me with him into the interior against my will . . .'

It was not the turnpike-keeper who reacted first, but one of the men who had tried to hire himself out to Judah.

'Blood and tare and 'ounds, miss! Mr Renshaw ain't no sharp! He's a square cove, and we all knows it!'

'What's yer game, miss?' another of the men demanded. 'Mr Renshaw's a real swell, a gent! He wouldn't do nothin' like what you just said!'

Judah himself merely sat impassively, as if the altercation did not involve him at all. Emerald ignored the other men, and again appealed to the turnpike-keeper.

'Please—you *must* help me! Even if you have no power to arrest him, at least make him set me down!'

The turnpike-keeper looked beyond her. 'What's to do, Jude?' he enquired with puzzled amusement. 'Why is the lady pitching me this wild tale?'

Dear lord, Emerald thought with despair, *did everyone in this whole benighted colony know and respect Judah Renshaw and automatically absolve him from any wrong-doing?*

She listened defeatedly as Judah launched into a smooth explanation.

'I believe I mentioned to you, didn't I, Harry, that I intended going to the bride-auction this trip. Well, I laid out twenty gold sovereigns for the lady.'

The turnpike-keeper whistled. 'That's steep!'

Judah gave Emerald a sidelong look. 'I thought she was worth a top price. I had her fitted out with a new wardrobe at O'Connors', and then took her to the George Hotel for a celebration luncheon. I think that was where I made my mistake, Harry. Having had a taste of the civilised life the colony has to offer, she decided that the interior was not for her after all.'

'That isn't true!' Emerald cried furiously.

'You're claiming Mr Renshaw didn't lay out good money for you, miss?'

'No, but . . .'

'Pay no heed, Harry,' Judah interrupted, and winked. 'After a week or two with me on Coorabee she'll be content enough to settle.'

The turnpike-keeper grinned, and moved to open the gate. 'You *must* help me!' Emerald cried with desperation. 'I have no intention of marrying Judah Renshaw, and I'm afraid of travelling into the interior with him, alone and at his mercy . . .'

At this, all the men burst into ribald laughter, and when it subsided the turnpike-keeper said mildly, 'No need to be afraid, miss, since he means to make an honest woman of you.'

Judah cracked his whip, drowning any other plea

Emerald might have attempted, and the dray lumbered through the gateway. One of the men shouted after them with irreverent humour,

'I only forked out five sovereigns for my Bess, Mr Renshaw, sir, and I reckon I got the better bargain, even if poor Bess ain't no high-steppin' red-headed beauty like what *you* bid for!'

In a voice throbbing with fury and repugnance, Emerald burst out, 'You are all savages in this place—worse than animals! One can scarcely believe that we are in the eighteen-thirties! Good God, even slavery has been abolished in the British colonies, and yet you all take it quite for granted that wives should be bought like livestock and treated in the same way . . .'

'Listen, Miss Morally-Outraged Travers,' Judah interrupted her in an abrasive voice. 'If *you* had been a genuine, impoverished female immigrant instead of a fraud, you might well have seen matters in a different light! If you had travelled to the colony to seek employment because it was your only escape from grinding poverty, how do you imagine *you* might have reacted if it had been suggested that you should allow yourself to be auctioned as a bride instead? Think of the alternatives—a choice between skivvying for someone else, or mistress of your own domain, however humble. Which would you have chosen?'

'I would *never* have sold myself in marriage to some unknown savage backwoodsman!'

'Those savage backwoodsmen, as you call them, are for the most part honest hard-working fellows who have no other means of finding themselves wives except by attending a bride-auction on a rare visit to Sydney. And these marriages turn out remarkably successfully, because each partner has cause to be grateful to the other!'

She gave him a withering look, but compressed her lips and said nothing. He did not trouble to break the ensuing silence between them, but gave his attention to the road.

It was rough, in places scarcely more than a track, and meandered over many a high exposed hill upon which the sun beat fiercely down.

At dusk Judah bellowed a command to the bullocks, and they halted in their shafts. Judah spoke for the first time.

'This will make a comfortable shake-down,' he said briskly.

Emerald guessed that he meant they were to camp there for the night, and her heart lurched with fear. There was no sign of civilisation, of another human being, around them. No one at all to protect her from the vengeance of Judah Renshaw; nowhere to run to. The few massive trees by which the dray had halted provided the only cover for miles, and the rest of the terrain was covered in scrub.

She remained in her seat, and watched as Judah removed an axe from the back of the dray. Skilfully he peeled bark from the trees, and soon had a fire going. He filled a tin can with water and placed it on the fire, and while he waited for it to boil he mixed flour and water in another receptacle, forming the dough into flat cakes which, after a while, he placed at the edge of the fire, on the ashes.

When the water was boiling he stripped a few leaves from one of the trees and flung them, together with a handful of tea, into the can. Then, with an indifferent glance at Emerald, he said, 'If you want tea and damper you'd better come down from there.'

She was beginning to feel a little ridiculous, perched obstinately in her seat. Not only that, but the evening air had acquired a distinct chill, and the fire looked inviting. He did not offer to help her as she climbed down from the dray.

She sat as far as possible from him, eating the flat rounds of baked dough which he called damper, and drinking her tea. It was a surprisingly appetising repast, and the leaves which he had tossed into the tea gave it a curious flavour.

She cleared her throat, and spoke for the first time since her enraged outburst. 'Are these eucalyptus trees?'

He nodded. 'We call them blue-gums. If you'll empty the billy-can and rinse it with water from the canteen, I'll go and cut some scrub to keep the fire going.'

Emerald had to remind herself forcibly that the tranquil, almost domestic scene was no more than an illusion. After Judah had returned with armfuls of scrub for the fire he reached in the back of the dray and brought out what looked like bed-rolls. Her stomach contracted with apprehension as he laid them out side by side near the fire.

She forced herself to speak steadily. 'If one of those is intended for me, I'll find my own sleeping-place, thank you.'

In the firelight his smile gave him the look of a satyr. 'Suit yourself.'

She picked up one bed-roll and moved to the other side of the fire, close to the trees. She stretched herself out on it, and her heart began to pound wildly when she saw Judah moving towards her, but he merely flung a possum-skin rug over her and said briefly, 'Sleep well.'

The words had been a mockery, for he must have known that sleep was the one thing she would not dare to indulge in. But as she lay there, taut with apprehension and poised for instant flight, it gradually began to dawn on her that he had no intention of approaching her. Indeed, she could hear his even breathing coming from the opposite side of the fire. Slowly she allowed herself to relax.

She was drifting into a doze when the night air was rent by the most hideous, indescribable noises close by. She let out a shrill sound of terror, and scrambled to her feet, grabbing up her bedding.

The light from the dying fire showed her that Judah was awake, leaning on one elbow and grinning mockingly. 'Come to join me after all, Miss Emerald Travers?'

'There's—something out there among the trees, and you are the only one with a gun . . .'

'Indeed.'

The fearful noises came again, and Emerald threw her bed-roll down as close as possible to Judah's. 'What . . . what are they?' she enquired between chattering teeth.

'Dingoes. A kind of wild dog. They're scavenging for any scraps we might have thrown out.' He reached for his carbine and fired a shot in the direction of the trees, and the dingoes ran off, yelping and growling.

'Now,' Judah asked with weary patience, 'would you mind settling down so that we may get some sleep?'

He was so close to her that he could have stretched out an arm and pulled her to him. But he turned on his side, and within a few minutes his even breathing again filled the silent night air.

Bewildered and perplexed, Emerald lay awake for some time beside him before she, too, drifted into sleep.

She awakened when dawn was streaking the horizon with rose and gold. Judah had already risen, and was boiling water for tea in the billy-can, and baking the inevitable damper. He greeted her with a slightly sardonic smile, but made no comment upon the events of the night, and after they had eaten and he had made sure the fire was completely doused, they continued the journey.

The track became even rougher, sometimes covered with long, coarse grass which threatened to trip up the bullocks; it took them through wild gullies and dry creeks, and suddenly altered dramatically when they reached an area where a nearby river had recently overflowed its banks. Here the dray became bogged down to the axles, sometimes one wheel going down so suddenly that Emerald thought they were in danger of overturning.

That night they had perforce to make camp in a large hollow depression surrounded by trees, through which the track had been leading for some distance.

After they had eaten, Judah laid the two bedrolls down side by side. He waited, his arms folded and a glint in his eyes, for her to protest, but Emerald said nothing. Instead, she pulled the rug over her and settled down to sleep.

But it was oppressively humid in that depression, the heat of the day having been trapped by the surrounding trees. Those same trees also obscured the sky so that the darkness was absolute once the fire had burnt out.

Emerald flung off the rug, but still found the humidity too uncomfortable to allow her to sleep. Judah Renshaw, in his lighter clothing and no doubt because he was accustomed to such conditions, had no such problems.

After a while, reassured by the sound of his even breathing and by the darkness, Emerald unbuttoned the bodice of her gown and shrugged her arms out of the sleeves, so that the upper part of her body was clothed only in her low-cut sleeveless chemise. Only then, her arms flung over her head for comfort, was she able to drift into sleep.

She was awakened, what seemed like minutes later, by an excruciating irritation of her skin. As she clawed vainly at her flesh for relief, she realised her own folly. That humid depression in the earth, in such proximity to the river, was infested with mosquitoes which had been happily feasting on her exposed skin.

'What the devil are you doing?' she heard Judah's voice demand with sleep-drugged irritation.

'Nothing.'

'You are doing it with considerable noise and a good deal of disturbing movement! Will you kindly remain silent and still, so that I may get back to sleep?'

She tried to obey, but the compulsion to scratch at the insect bites was too overwhelming, and even though she tried to be surreptitious and quiet about it, Judah uttered a sudden oath, and she heard him rising.

'If you have an itch in some inaccessible place,

Miss Travers, then for heaven's sake let me scratch it for you so that we may both gain some relief!'

'It . . . it isn't merely an itch,' she confessed. 'I . . . removed some of my clothing because of the humidity, and I've been bitten all over by mosquitoes . . .'

He laughed unsympathetically. 'Idiot! It serves you right. Didn't you have the sense to realise that conditions like these are a breeding-ground for mosquitoes, and that you should remain covered?'

'I realise it now,' she returned tersely, 'and I *have* covered myself, but that only serves to make the irritation worse.'

'I have some ointment on the dray,' he said. 'I'll do my best to find it.'

She listened as he moved towards the dray and searched among its contents with the aid of a lighted lucifer match. Then she was aware of him feeling his way back to the bed-rolls.

She could see only the dim outlines of his face as he crouched over her. 'Kindly remove whatever it was you removed before, Miss Travers, so that I may apply the ointment,' he commanded.

She cringed away from him. 'No! I'll apply it myself.'

'I have no intention,' he told her roughly, 'of lying and listening to the maddening sound of you squirming about as you try to reach the insect bites.' A mocking note entered his voice. 'It is far too dark for me to gain more than a faint impression of your no-doubt delectable body, so you can have no objections on that score.'

'I . . . If you will just give the ointment to me . . .'

His manner turned rough. 'I am extremely tired,

Miss Travers, and not in the mood for your girlish airs. If you do not remove those garments yourself, I shall do it for you!'

She had no alternative but to obey, with shaking hands. She lay rigidly, and tried not to cringe in fear as he began to apply ointment first to her arms and shoulders, his movements methodical and brisk to begin with but altering as he started to work on her throat. By the time he had reached the area just above her breasts his hands were no longer brisk, but moved lingeringly, almost caressingly, over her skin.

She was shaken by two totally conflicting emotions warring inside her. One was an excited awareness of him which deeply shamed her, and the other was fear.

This, surely, was the moment when he would punish her and take revenge against Andrew by ravishing her . . .

His hands ceased their slow movements and became still. Then one finger traced a line along the hollow between her breasts, very lightly, and she lay quivering in the darkness, a strange languor invading her body so that she knew she would not have the strength to fight him when he made the next, inevitable move.

To her astonishment and bafflement, however, he sat back on his haunches and said briskly, 'Now replace your clothing, and go to sleep. I don't wish to hear another sound from you until morning, Miss Travers!'

He returned to his own bed-roll, and she puzzled over his behaviour during the brief moments before she fell asleep, her skin miraculously soothed by the ointment.

He was, it was beginning to seem, playing with her as a cat plays with a mouse.

Once again, in the morning, he made no reference to what had happened and they continued their journey. When they reached higher ground Emerald could see that the horizon was outlined by hills enveloped in a brilliant blue-tinted haze.

That night, instead of making camp in the open, they stopped at a solitary wayside inn. It was a crude wooden construction built on stilts, with a veranda running all round it.

'Wait here,' Judah commanded, 'while I go and see whether Bartholomew Grant is able to offer us a meal and accommodation.'

The thought of a proper bed in which to sleep was inviting, and so was the prospect of a change from tea and damper. But far more important, cheerful voices were coming from inside the inn, and there was a good chance that she might be able to appeal to one of the other guests to save her from Judah Renshaw.

The war of nerves which he was waging with her was becoming too tense for her to bear, and someone in the inn might have the authority to force Renshaw to leave her there while a message was sent to Andrew to come and collect her.

But that had been a vain hope, as she realised a while later when Judah steered her into what appeared to be a large tap-room. Far from having any authority, the men crowded inside appeared to be ordinary rough labourers. They clearly knew Judah and regarded him with deference and respect; moreover, most of them were obviously inebriated.

Emerald realised, at a glance, that she could

expect no help either from the fawning landlord, or from the sullen-looking girl whom he commanded curtly, 'See to the lady, you!'

The girl led the way through the tap-room, picking her way over barrels of beer and kegs of rum, and opened a door, standing silently aside for Emerald to enter.

The bedroom was large and devoid of comfort, containing only a bed and a rickety table. Moreover, it looked none too clean.

'Are all the bedrooms like this?' Emerald asked with dismay.

The girl uttered a grim laugh. '*All*? This 'ere's the only one there is!'

'But—all those other guests—where on earth do *they* sleep?'

Stunned, Emerald listened as the girl explained that it was a communal room, normally shared by all guests staying at the inn. Whoever shared the bed paid a higher price, and the rest of the men slept in ranks on the floor.

But tonight Judah Renshaw had come to a special arrangement with the proprietor, and he had compensated the other guests. Emerald listened with numb despair as the girl explained, 'The room's for you and the gennelman only. The others'll doss down on the veranda.' She added ungraciously, 'I'm to fetch yer supper to you now.'

Emerald was prowling around the room when the girl returned with a pannikin of tea and a cold mutton pie and pickles. She was about to leave again, but Emerald said desperately,

'Wait! Are you the landlord's daughter?'

'*Daughter*!' Again the girl gave a brief, bitter laugh. 'I'm a lag, miss, a convict. I works for 'im. I does as I'm told; I keeps me mouf shut and minds me own business. That way, I stand less chance of gettin' a beltin'—or worse, of losin' me ticket.'

For the first time, Emerald looked properly at the girl and noticed the fading bruises on her cheek, her air of sullen resignation and numb endurance.

It all served to make her feel ashamed of her own self-preoccupation. Whatever the girl had done to cause herself to be transported, her present situation must be truly wretched. It would be morally indefensible as well as useless to appeal to her to involve herself with Emerald's affairs.

When she was alone once more, Emerald's first action was to fly to the door and see whether it could be secured against Judah Renshaw. But, as she had feared, there was no key. Neither was there anything in the room which could have been used as a barricade.

She sat on the edge of the lumpy bed and ate her supper. From the tap-room she could hear the revelry of the other guests. But gradually the noises began to diminish and she could hear the thumping sounds the men made as they settled themselves to sleep off their excesses on the wooden veranda.

She crouched like an animal at bay against the headboard of the bed, watching the door. But no attempt was made to open it. How far did Judah Renshaw mean to take this cat-and-mouse game he was playing with her, torturing her with uncertainty—obviously as part of his plan for revenge?

She felt her eyelids grow heavy, but was instantly alert again when she heard a sound outside the door. She waited, her muscles tense. Nothing more happened.

When she judged that at least an hour must have

gone by, she rose silently, and picking up the branch of candles, padded to the door. Very slowly and carefully she turned the knob and pulled the door towards her, and then caught her breath with astonishment.

Judah Renshaw lay fast asleep on his bed-roll outside the door, his carbine beside him, exactly as if he were on guard.

On guard against what? She closed the door again carefully. He could not possibly fear that she might try to escape from him during the night, here in the middle of nowhere.

She frowned as she pondered the enigma. This was the third night when he could, without the slightest difficulty, have forced himself upon her, and yet he had failed to do so. It was not lack of desire which was holding him back either; she knew that. In spite of his brusque tone last night when he had applied the ointment to her skin, the pressure of his fingers had revealed only too plainly his physical awareness of her.

And tonight, no one in the bush inn had had the slightest doubt that he meant to share with her the only bed for hire. He had paid for its exclusive use and had let it be known that it was to be occupied by the two of them. And yet he was lying asleep outside the door, with his bed-roll spread on the hard floor and his carbine at his hand . . .

The answer came to her quite suddenly. He *was* on guard; he was protecting her from molestation by one of the drunken guests who, if Judah had shared the veranda with them, would almost certainly have blundered to her room.

Why was he protecting her when he had sworn vengeance against her? Why had he made no attempt to humiliate and ravish her, as she had expected?

'I'm going to take you to Andrew Standish,' he had said, *'and believe me, you will be wishing with all your heart that I had left you to starve in Sydney instead.'*

So he must be planning to take his revenge *after* he had delivered her safely to Andrew. She brought out the bundle of letters, and began to read them again, searching for clues which would have meant nothing to her at the time.

After he had left Wallalong, Andrew had written, *'You will see from the address, my dearest, that I am now farming at a place called Coorabee Creek. While the work is just as hard as before, and the rewards no higher, there are certain compensations. I am no longer quite as solitary as I was at Wallalong, where I had to rely solely on my "tame" Aboriginal stockmen for company. Here, at least, there are other white people, and even if some of them tend to mistrust a "new chum" such as myself, and there is at least one who would be quite happy to see me ruined and defeated . . . Well, as I've said, there are compensations, notwithstanding.'*

Thoughtfully, Emerald re-folded the letter. Andrew could not have been referring to anyone other than Judah Renshaw, even though none of his subsequent letters had mentioned the man's enmity.

She had already been made to realise that Judah was a powerful man in the district, that he was respected and deferred to. And Andrew was a new immigrant, trying to gain a foothold in the colony. She could now see, quite clearly, how Judah meant to exact his revenge. He would take her to Andrew, and then wait until they were married before he set about ruining and defeating her beloved. And her own punishment would lie in the knowledge that she had been the cause of it all.

After breakfast the next morning, they continued their journey. As before, Judah scrupulously kept his distance, and when they spoke at all it was about generalities. He explained to her that the hills they were approaching derived their mist-blue colouring from the forests of blue-gum trees which overspread the valleys and heights, and were the foothills of the Blue Mountains.

That night, after they had eaten their supper, Emerald asked abruptly, 'Why do you hate Andrew?'

Judah's eyes hardened, as they always did at a mention of her fiancé. 'It makes my gorge rise to talk about it. You'll learn soon enough, in any case, when you have married him. *If* you marry him.' He added tauntingly, 'He does not strike me as a particularly ardent groom, since he did not even trouble to meet your ship.'

'I believe we have *you* to thank for that!' Emerald said heatedly. 'I've little doubt that you collected my letter to Andrew that announced my arrival, and maliciously destroyed it!'

'My dear girl, there is never anything *petty* about my revenge! I would annihilate and destroy my enemy—I wouldn't trouble to tamper with his mail.'

'In that case, the letter must have gone astray.'

Judah shrugged, indicating that he did not wish to discuss the subject any further, and spread out the bed-rolls so that they could sleep.

At mid-morning the following day, Emerald demanded, 'How much longer do we have to travel before we reach Coorabee Creek?'

'We've reached it. We have been on Coorabee land for the past two hours.'

She stared about her. There was nothing whatever about the landscape to distinguish it from any other they had been travelling through since leaving Sydney, except that the foothills of the Blue Mountains now dominated the scene. But there had been nothing to mark any boundaries.

'I saw no sign-posts,' she argued.

Judah gave a short laugh. 'This is not England, Miss Travers. Everyone within a hundred miles' radius knows where Coorabee begins and ends, and strangers rarely come this way.'

'How far are we from your farm?' she wanted to know.

'Station,' he corrected. 'We still have several hours' drive ahead of us before we reach the homestead.'

When they did reach it, Emerald saw that it was a well-built house of weatherboard with a veranda on all sides. Surrounding it were outbuildings which Judah informed her were the barns, shearing sheds, cart-houses and labourers' huts. A well-laid-out kitchen garden spread away from the house.

As the dray stopped outside it, a young woman, plainly dressed but of a quite startling dark beauty, came out of the house to meet them, dragging two patently unwilling children by the hand.

The boy was about eight years old, his sister perhaps two years younger. They gazed at Emerald with hard, hostile eyes.

'How have they been, Alice?' Judah asked the dark-haired beauty.

'About the same.' She glanced at Emerald and flushed, and added as an obvious and unfamiliar afterthought, 'Mr Renshaw.'

Judah turned to Emerald. 'I'd like to present Timothy and Selina . . .'

Before he could continue, the boy interrupted to demand of Emerald, 'Are you to be our new auntie?'

'No . . .'

'I'm glad!' Timothy cried fiercely. 'Selina is glad too. We don't like you, any more than we like Alice! We want to go home!'

'You know that isn't possible,' Judah said helplessly, and for a moment he appeared to Emerald to be vulnerable and at a loss.

He transferred his attention to her. 'If you would care to go inside the house with Alice, the servants will offer you refreshments . . .'

'I'd rather not, thank you. Is Andrew's place very far from here?'

'About an hour's drive with a fresh team of horses.'

The girl, Alice, looked both bewildered and relieved. 'Murphy could drive the lady,' she suggested to Judah.

'No, this is something I wish to attend to myself,' he said grimly. 'I'll go and hitch the team to the wagonette.'

He strode away. Emerald reached into the back of the dray for her carpet-bags and then alighted and waited. Judah reappeared from one of the outbuildings with the wagonette, and soon the two of them were driving away, watched by Alice and the stony-faced children.

Emerald wondered who Alice was, and why

Judah had been prepared to buy a wife for himself if she was already installed in his house and caring for the children. Then she dismissed them from her mind as excitement gripped her. Very soon now she would be reunited with Andrew . . .

She was astonished when their destination came into view. None of Andrew's letters had hinted that he had acquired such a fine house for himself, with such extensive outbuildings. Indeed, she would have said that his homestead was superior to Judah's. There was even a flower garden beside one of the verandas.

As she gathered her carpet-bags together, Judah withdrew a bundle of mail from his pocket and dropped it inside her reticule. 'You may as well deliver this.'

He helped her from the wagonette and returned to his seat, but his attitude made it plain that he had no intention of driving away immediately. 'I suppose,' Emerald said coldly, 'you are waiting for your twenty sovereigns to be repaid.'

He merely inclined his head, and she was aware that he was watching her as she mounted the steps to the veranda.

A servant wearing livery of blue nankeen cloth met her at the door, and responded respectfully when she asked for Andrew. Emerald's head was spinning. Andrew—with liveried servants tending to his needs?

And then, suddenly, the door of the pleasantly appointed living-room into which she had been shown opened, and they were face to face after their long parting.

He had not changed. He was still fine-boned and clean-shaven, with the gentle good looks she remembered and loved so well. He had acquired a tan, but his face had paled beneath it at the shock of seeing her, and his brown eyes had a blank look as though he were staring at a ghost.

He stood frozen into immobility. At last he said in a numb monotone, 'It . . . it isn't possible . . .'

'Oh, Andrew, my dearest!' She sped across the room and flung her arms about his neck. 'It really is me! You didn't get my letter, did you?'

'Letter . . . ? No. No, I didn't, Emerald.'

'Aren't you going to kiss me?' she asked softly, reaching up to him.

He took her offered mouth, but his reactions were like those of a man in a hypnotic trance. He lifted his head, and mumbled, 'I'm—sorry. I can't . . .'

'You have nothing to apologise for, my love,' Emerald said gently. 'I am not pettish enough to expect ardour from a man who is clearly suffering from shock.'

'You—have always been so wonderfully understanding.' His voice sounded mechanical.

'Come, let us sit down, Andrew, and I'll tell you how it came about that I was able to join you so much sooner than we had hoped, and after a while you will lose the feeling that I am a figment of your imagination!'

He tried to smile in response. 'I think—perhaps a large measure of rum will answer the case better. And some tea for you—I dare say you would welcome a dish of tea? I'll attend to the matter . . .'

There seemed to be something like desperation about the way in which he hurried from the room. Almost as if he were fleeing, trying to gain time . . .

Nonsense, Emerald told herself firmly. Her sudden appearance from out of the blue had disoriented him completely, and thrown him off balance, so that he was scarcely aware of what he was doing. Why, otherwise, had he not rung for the liveried servant to bring his drink and her tea?

She frowned as she remembered the servant, and the indications of unsuspected wealth all around her. Uncomfortable questions surged into her mind, but she quelled them swiftly. Andrew would explain everything in due time.

While she waited for him to return, Emerald reached into her reticule for the parcel of mail and, as she pulled it out, the string became undone, spilling the letters on the floor. Emerald was gathering them up when she discovered, with astonishment, that one of them was a small package addressed to herself. She recognised Nanny's handwriting, and realised that her old nurse must have written to her after she had left for Plymouth and that the package had obviously travelled out to the colony on the *Aurora* with her.

The package consisted of a letter, and a covering note from Nanny, explaining that it had arrived only hours after Emerald left London for Plymouth. The letter had been addressed to her by Andrew.

Breaking its seal, she skimmed its contents, her mouth growing dry with shock and a terrible glimmering of understanding. Andrew *had* received her letter, and this was his reply to it.

'*Of course I long for you to join me,*' he had written, '*but not yet, my dearest. The homestead is no more than a hovel . . . not fit for any female . . . no decent facilities . . . Invest your legacy . . . What-*

ever you do, don't make the voyage until you hear from me again . . .'

Emerald refolded the letter with exaggerated care, as if it were the most important task in the world. She looked around her at the comfortably appointed room with its furniture which must have been shipped from England.

A *hovel*? Not fit for any female? What other lies had Andrew been telling her in his letters?

The sound of footsteps mounting the stairs to the veranda reached her, and Emerald heard a woman's voice, throaty and eager and intimate.

'Darling, that's Judah outside! I could scarcely believe . . .'

'He has brought Emerald.' Andrew sounded distraught. 'Damn him, he has obviously told her nothing! How in God's name am I to explain to her . . .'

Feeling as if she had been mortally wounded, Emerald moved slowly until she could look out of the window on to the western side of the veranda, from which the voices had come.

A slim, pretty woman with corn-coloured hair stood close beside Andrew, her left hand on his arm in a proprietary gesture. The afternoon sunshine glinted on the plain gold band which she wore on her third finger.

The world seemed to explode around Emerald. She found herself running from the room, from the house, leaping down the veranda steps, ignoring Andrew's cries to her to wait.

Judah leant out of the driving seat of the wagonette to help her up. She turned on him, beating impotently against his chest with her fists, the tears flowing down her cheeks.

'You—*devil*,' she gasped. 'Evil, despicable, malicious devil . . . You knew . . . knew what was awaiting me . . . Oh, you *fiend* . . .'

He imprisoned her fists in his hand, and held her for a moment. Then he released her and picked up the reins.

Without expression, he said, 'Come, I'm taking you home.'

CHAPTER THREE

EMERALD SAT huddled in her seat, her face covered by her hands. The aggression had left her and now there were only grief and pain coursing through her, taking her over completely. Judah concentrated on driving, cracking his whip in the air with unnecessary force.

After they had been driving for some minutes, he suddenly pulled at the reins and the vehicle came to a halt. He sat in silence beside her while she wept, and once made an attempt to place a comforting arm about her shoulder. She thrust him violently aside. He did not try to touch her again.

At last she succeeded in gaining some control over herself, and fumbled inside her reticule for a handkerchief. 'Now that you know the truth,' she heard Judah say, 'you can, perhaps, understand the depth of my scorn and hatred for Andrew Standish. The trouble with his sort is that they don't appear to be rogues, devoid of honour or principles. They lull one into trusting them . . .'

'*Shut up!*' Emerald whispered fiercely through clenched teeth. 'What you did was almost as bad!'

'Yes,' he agreed unexpectedly, his voice flat. 'I thought I would savour my revenge to the full. If it gives you any comfort at all, I have found that I was wrong. And, in my own defence, perhaps I should add that I would not have been so bent on revenge in the first place if my disappointment in you had not been quite so acute. Andrew Standish is not only a rogue, but also . . .'

'I don't want to hear!' Emerald interrupted in a fiery tone. 'You deliberately chose not to tell me that he had married someone else. You allowed me to come all this way . . .' Her voice broke. 'So—now be quiet and leave me alone!'

He opened his mouth to say something more, but she clapped her hands to her ears. Then he shrugged, and picked up the reins once more, and did not speak again.

She stared ahead of her, mechanically taking in the landscape. Stunted scrub was broken up, here and there, by large blue-gums or white cedar trees between which brightly coloured birds flitted. One species of bird emitted a cry which sounded like mocking, hysterical laughter, as though it were commenting on Emerald's situation, on the cruel death of all her hopes.

How *could* Andrew have done such a thing to her?

Only a short year ago, he had loved her enough to defy his family, at the cost of being cut off with a shilling by his wealthy father. He had taken up a grant of land in the colony, starting with little more in the way of assets than any other common immigrant—all so that he could send for her and marry her. What had happened to change everything?

She remembered his first letters, from Wallalong, in which he had described the lack of all material comforts, the unremitting hardness of the work, the pitifully scant return for all his labour. The contrast between that description and what she had seen at Coorabee Creek could not have been more marked.

There was only one possible, logical explanation which fitted. Without telling her, Andrew must have become reconciled with his father. Perhaps the hardness of the life at Wallalong had forced him to pocket his pride and his principles and write to his father for financial help.

And with that financial help he had bought the property at Coorabee Creek. But there would have been a price to pay, of course. Andrew's father would never have sent him money if there had been the remotest possibility that he might marry Emerald. So, he would have insisted on a 'suitable' marriage to a 'suitable' girl.

Emerald's mouth twisted bitterly. The pretty fair-haired girl wearing Andrew's wedding ring had certainly appeared to be the kind of wife his father would have deemed suitable. In all probability she was someone from Andrew's social set in England, one of the many girls he had squired to balls and soirées before he fell in love with Emerald. The match had been arranged by their respective parents, and as a reward Andrew's father had paid for the well-appointed station. It went without saying that the girl had also brought a substantial dowry with her from England, not to mention the quality furniture and the fancy livery for the servants . . .

Once again Emerald's thoughts were punctuated by that mocking bird-cry. 'It's a kookaburra, a laughing jackass,' Judah explained, seeing her wince.

She made no response. *Why*, her mind was persisting painfully, had Andrew continued to write her those loving, lying letters after he had married someone else?

There could be only one answer. He was basically a kind man who could not bear to hurt anyone. And so he had been unable to bring himself to tell Emerald the truth. Perhaps he had hoped that a prolonged parting would change her own feelings, that she would transfer them to someone else, and so spare him the need to hurt her.

'*Judah has brought Emerald,*' Andrew had confided to his wife, and had added distractedly, 'How in God's name am I to explain to her?'

Something else stirred among the welter of pain and misery clouding Emerald's mind. It was anger and a sense of bitter humiliation. Andrew's wife had obviously known all about her, had probably even helped him to compose those letters to her. This was, perhaps, the greatest betrayal of all, and something which Emerald found almost impossible to endure or ever to forgive.

She shook her head blindly. It was no use going over and over the reasons and motives for everything that had happened. She had to decide what she was to do about her immediate future.

Andrew would probably be only too eager to give her the money for her return passage to England, and was no doubt at that very moment discussing with his wife how Emerald could be compensated for her wasted journey and for the shock and pain of her discovery. The very thought made her cringe.

She would not accept a penny from Andrew. That would be the final humiliation, something with which she could not live. And yet, what other alternatives were open to her? She was stranded and destitute. She was already in debt to Judah Renshaw . . .

A sound midway between a sob and a harsh laugh escaped her. With what arrogant confidence she had looked to Andrew to repay that debt!

No, she could not accept money from Andrew, no matter how much he might wish to salve his conscience by offering it to her, no matter how eagerly he and his wife might want to be rid of her embarrassing presence, no matter where else she might have to turn.

She glanced at Judah beside her, and reflected with searing vengefulness how extremely uncomfortable and mortifying it would be for Andrew if she *were* to marry Judah, and remain there on his doorstep as a constant reminder of what he had done to her . .

She came to a swift and impulsive decision, and broke the silence. 'Would you still consider me a suitable candidate for a marriage of convenience, a fit person to bring up your sister's children?'

He turned his head and gave her a slow, sidelong look. 'Eminently suitable.'

'In that case,' she said with sour humour, 'since you have invested twenty sovereigns in me, and Andrew is already married so that I can no longer look to him to reimburse you, I shall strive to give value for money.'

He did not do or say anything to soften the harshly mercenary terms in which she had phrased her promise to marry him. He merely gave an unsmiling nod, and said, 'I fear you will have trouble with the children to begin with, but you will doubtless already have realised that.'

'Yes.' She tried to banish thoughts of Andrew

and his fair-haired bride from her mind, and to concentrate on the children instead. 'They grieve for their parents. You said your sister and her husband had been killed. How did it happen?'

'Their farmhouse was attacked by Aborigines and set on fire. Mary, my sister, and her husband were both trapped in the blazing house. A convict servant had spirited the children out of the house at the beginning of the attack, and thus saved their lives.'

'It is little wonder that they are difficult, after such a terrible experience,' Emerald commented.

'Yes.' There was a note of constraint in his voice.

Something else occurred to her. 'Who and what is Alice?' she demanded.

'A convict servant.'

'Oh . . . The same one who saved the children's lives?'

'No. That particular girl has since been given a conditional pardon, and has married another ex-convict and moved away. Alice is working her ticket as my housekeeper.'

'I see . . .' Emerald saw only too well. She remembered the wretched little convict girl in the bush inn, and contrasted her with Alice. Apparently in the colony the fate of a convict depended more on the people for whom they were forced to work than on the terms and duration of their servitude.

Clearly, Alice had been Judah's mistress. Everything about the girl had confirmed that impression—the way in which she had called him 'Mr Renshaw' as an afterthought; her undisguised relief when she learnt that Emerald was not, after all, to be Judah's bride.

If she had needed any further evidence, Emerald only had to recall Judah's own statements. '*I have no intention of having my sister's children hurt,*' he had told her in Sydney, '*by any slurs cast upon the character of the woman who has the care of them.*'

There must have been local gossip and criticism about the children being brought up by Judah's convict-mistress, and that was why he had decided to acquire a wife.

'What did Alice do to cause her to be transported?' Emerald asked aloud.

'She was found guilty of the manslaughter of her husband.'

'Oh!'

'He was a drunken brute who misused her, and she acted in self-defence. But people here are not concerned with mitigating circumstances. For the rest of her life, even after she has worked her ticket, she will have to bear the slur of her conviction.'

So there had been local criticism, Emerald thought. And the swiftness with which he had minimised Alice's crime clearly showed that he regarded her as much more than just another convict and servant.

'*I have never had to pay for a woman,*' Judah had said at their first meeting, '*and I shall have no need to do so in the future if you should insist on keeping our marriage on a platonic plane.*'

What could that have meant, other than that he had had a mistress who would be only too ready to resume that role if she were asked to?

Well, Emerald thought coldly, that arrangement would suit herself very well. She had no intention of pretending to cast Andrew from her heart and her mind, and submitting to the charade of being

Judah's wife in every sense of the word. After all, there was only so much he could expect in return for twenty sovereigns and her keep. She would care for his sister's children and do her best to supervise his household, and that would be all.

But the outside world would never know it. Judah was far too proud a man for that. *Andrew* would never know it. He must have some feeling left for her—a feeling which would be fanned by her continued nearness and which would cause him to regret, more and more, his arranged marriage. How richly he deserved to be harrowed by the thought that she spent her nights in the arms of his enemy . . .

Raw bitterness and a desire for revenge caused her to say, 'Since we are to be married, I trust it will be possible to get it over and done with soon.'

'We'll drive to the courthouse in the morning.' His tone was as businesslike and unemotional as her own.

A spasm crossed her face as she remembered how she had pictured in her mind her marriage to Andrew. Not in some bleak bush courthouse, but in a church in Sydney, wearing the rose-coloured percale gown which would have brought back so many poignant memories for him . . .

Practical reality suddenly cut through her musing, and she made a sound of dismay. 'We shall have to go back to Andrew's place!' she exclaimed. 'I have left my carpet-bags behind!'

'It has been a long day,' Judah responded curtly, 'and we are three-quarters of the way home. I have no intention of turning back now.'

'But the bags contain everything I possess, apart from what I am wearing at the moment! I cannot possibly wear them again tomorrow—not even for a mockery of a marriage in a courthouse! I have been travelling through the dusty bush in these clothes since daybreak!'

He gave her an indifferent glance. 'What an inordinate fuss women make about clothes! The servants will launder what you are wearing now, and it will all be fresh and clean for the morning. I'll send Murphy, my overseer, to collect your carpet-bags some time tomorrow.'

Emerald flushed, both with anger and embarrassment. 'I hardly imagine that you can realise what respectable young women wear underneath their gowns. *Those* garments will not be capable of being laundered overnight!'

'You are referring to your stays and pantaloons and petticoats, I suppose,' he said, a note of amusement in his voice. 'Well, I have never understood what practical purpose any of them serve.'

Her flush deepened. 'I shall have no night attire, either, unless we go back for my bags.'

'The nights out here are warm and balmy,' he interrupted. 'I, myself, have never felt the need for night attire of any kind unless I am camping in the bush.'

There was no point in allowing him to go on baiting her in this infuriating, taunting manner. Emerald compressed her lips and said no more. She would just have to wear damp clothing tomorrow for her wedding. With sudden, uncharacteristic morbid depression, she thought, *Perhaps I shall contract pneumonia and die, and that will be the end of my misery* . . .

It was not until they approached the station that Judah broke the silence once more, a note of irony in his voice. 'Allow me to introduce you properly to your new domain. To the left of us is the stockyard, where the horses are run in; beyond it is the slaughter-yard, the fowl-houses and piggeries and shearing sheds.'

Emerald could not even guess what it meant to 'run in' horses, but she felt that some show of interest was expected from her. 'Yours is a mixed farm?' she enquired politely.

'No. We keep pigs and cattle and poultry for food and dairy produce for our own use, but I have recently broken with tradition and sold off my cattle herds, bringing in sheep in their place. I see a great future for sheep out here.'

His voice had taken on a note of enthusiasm, and Emerald questioned him without having a remote interest in his answers. All she wanted was to keep thoughts of Andrew at bay, for she was mortally afraid of losing control of her feelings again.

As they drew to a halt outside the house, Judah cupped his hands about his mouth and shouted, 'Murphy!'

A large red-haired man with a ruddy complexion came hurrying from the direction of the outbuildings. 'Sor?' he addressed Judah in a heavy brogue.

'Please see to the horses.'

'To be sure I will, sor.' The overseer sketched a polite salute in Emerald's direction as he spoke. His eyes, she noticed, were a curious reddish-brown, reminding her of those of a fox.

The sun was setting, turning the edges and summits of the blue backdrop of mountains to a translucent rose. It also softened the house, and this time Emerald gave closer attention to it.

It was a single-storey construction with a veranda

all round. Although squat and sprawling, it appeared to offer accommodation comparable to a British farmhouse, and flowering vines and honeysuckle had been trained to climb the supports of the veranda and along the walls.

As before, Alice emerged from the front door, holding the two children by their hands, but this time the young ones were dressed in night-clothes.

Taking Emerald's arm, Judah squired her up the steps of the veranda. He addressed the children, making his voice determinedly cheerful, but Emerald did not miss the underlying note of uneasiness.

'This is Miss Emerald Travers, children. She has changed her mind, and is to be your new auntie after all, and will be taking care of you.'

Emerald had been watching Alice's face, and had seen the swift spasm which crossed it. She wished that convention could have made it possible for her to reassure the woman that she had nothing to fear, no reason for jealousy or for the same kind of desolation that Emerald was experiencing. But there was no way of letting Alice know that her marriage to Judah would be in name only, and so Emerald gave her attention to the children instead, holding out her hand to them. She noticed that Judah had drawn Alice to one side, and was talking to her in an undertone. Perhaps *he* was explaining matters to her.

The little girl, Selina, appeared to be on the point of taking Emerald's hand. But her brother Timothy said with deliberate rudeness, 'We don't want a new auntie! I shan't mind you or do what you say, and neither will Selina!'

'Don't want a new auntie,' Selina muttered,

taking her cue from her brother and drawing back.

Judah gave Emerald a helpless look. 'I'm sorry.'

Alice said resignedly, 'I'm afraid the children refused to be put to bed. They insisted on waiting for you—Mr Renshaw.'

He sighed. 'I'll go and see to them. Show Miss Travers the house, Alice, and then put her in the lilac room. Have someone draw a bath for her. I'm sure she would prefer to have her meal served in her room, and retire early.'

It was a command, not a suggestion. Emerald felt too listless and drained to whip up indignation at such high-handedness. Judah scooped Selina into his arms and took Timothy's hand, and entered the house.

Emerald shook her head. Seeing him with the children, and picturing him putting them to bed, conjured up a side of him which she had never suspected existed.

Then she shrugged the thought aside as Alice said in a strained voice, 'If you would care to follow me, Miss Travers.'

The house was entirely built of wood and the rooms were large, with lofty ceilings. Alice led the way first to the kitchen, which stood apart from the main building of the house and was connected to it by a veranda and a wide trellis of vines. Instead of a range, the kitchen boasted an enormous fireplace, with a shelf of cemented stones and two iron bars on which the saucepans rested. A round detachable pan with a lid buried almost entirely in hot coals obviously did service as an oven. A large shapeless woman whom Alice introduced as Hettie presided over the kitchen, helped by a young woman with sullen eyes and meagre sandy hair.

From the kitchen, Emerald was taken to inspect the dairy, which was partly underground and roofed with bark which had been laid over rafters and then covered with earth to keep it cool.

Alice was determined to carry out Judah's instructions to the letter, so that Emerald was forced to follow her to the meat-house with its large table at which the freshly butchered meat was being cut up by yet another young woman and then placed in casks of brine.

They made a tour which took in the office where Judah kept his accounts and his records at an oak desk, and where he stored his collection of guns. Then on to the two main living-rooms and the numerous bedrooms, most of which led straight out on to the veranda.

'This is the lilac room,' Alice said, opening one of the doors. The room derived its name from the colour of the curtains and bed-hangings, and was pleasant and cool-looking.

'It is a fine house,' Emerald commented, feeling that she was expected to say something enthusiastic after her tour of inspection.

'It is indeed, Miss Travers. Most station homesteads are no more than a hut with an earth floor, separated into two or three rooms.'

Anguish, sharp and terrible in its suddenness, tore through Emerald. It was just such a simple dwelling that she had envisaged as her journey's end. She had imagined living there with Andrew, gradually softening their drab surroundings with embroideries and patchwork lovingly laboured over while they sat together in the evenings . . .

What did she want, instead, with this fine house in which there was no love?

Oh Andrew, her heart cried out in grief. *How could you have sold what we might have had for the sake of another place just like this and a life of ease?*

Involuntary tears began to trickle down her cheeks, and even though she made no sound and kept her face averted from Alice, the latter said softly, 'You are homesick. It is natural.'

Emerald's control broke, and she found herself cradled in Alice's embrace. The girl held her in silence until the storm of weeping had abated.

Emerald lifted her head, and attempted a smile. 'I'm sorry.'

'There is no need to be, Miss Travers.'

Impulsively, speaking from a heartfelt need and an instinctive sense of affinity with this girl, Emerald said, 'Please let us be friends! Call me Emerald?'

'I could hardly do that,' Alice answered quietly. 'I am a convict, Miss Travers.'

Emerald was silent. Alice's dignity and her inherent gentility caused one to forget her true status. After a moment, mindful of the other servants she had met, she asked in a subdued voice, 'Hettie and the girls—are they convicts too?'

'They are.'

How strange and grotesque, Emerald thought, to be surrounded and served by convicted criminals . . .

Alice smiled wryly as though she understood precisely what Emerald was thinking, but she merely said, 'I shall arrange for your bath now, and have a tray sent in to you later, Miss Travers.'

A short while afterwards the two other convict girls carried a hip bath into the room and filled it with hot water. Emerald wondered what crimes they had committed, but instinct warned her not to ask. She retired behind a screen and stripped off her clothing, handing all but her chemise to the girls for laundering.

After they had withdrawn, she bathed and washed her hair, and then the girls returned to remove the bath and tidy the room. When she was alone once more, Emerald sat before the mirror, clad only in her chemise, and brushed her hair until it was dry and fell like a soft dark-red cloud about her face.

Someone knocked on the door, and she called out an invitation to enter, expecting it to be one of the girls with her tray. Instead, to her consternation and acute discomfiture, it was Judah, carrying something wrapped in tissue.

She jumped to her feet, crossing her arms about her breast, embarrassingly conscious of the absence of her stays to flatten and camouflage and distort her natural shape in accordance with the dictates of fashion and modesty.

'How . . . how dare you . . .' she began in a strangled voice.

His eyebrows rose. 'Why such maidenly outrage? Am I not entitled to gain some idea of what I am to get for my twenty sovereigns?'

Emerald was about to point out to him, in no uncertain terms, precisely what he would be getting for his twenty sovereigns. But then he disarmed her by dropping his taunting manner, and saying simply,

'I've brought you something to wear at your wedding tomorrow. It was my mother's; she treasured it greatly because my father bought it for her when he could least afford it. I know it would have pleased her to have you wear it.'

He unwrapped the tissue and held the gown out for Emerald's inspection. She stared at it in dismay. It was simple and quite charming, of white muslin cut low at the front and decorated with blue ribbon threaded below the bust, but it belonged to another era, to another mode of fashion. How could she tell him that it would be quite impossible for her to wear his mother's treasured gown?

'Put it on,' Judah commanded.

'I . . . this is most unseemly . . .'

'I had not expected coyness of you, Emerald! We are to be married tomorrow, after all, and for purely practical reasons it is necessary that you should try on the gown. If it does not fit, Alice will have to be asked to modify it for you. I'll turn my back, if that would satisfy your modesty.'

'Very well,' Emerald gave in helplessly.

The gown, in spite of its simplicity, was quite shocking by modern standards. Apart from the lowness of its draped neckline, it had not been designed to be worn over any of the current confining stays or hoops or many petticoats, but clung quite shamelessly to the natural curves of Emerald's body.

Judah turned around and moved slowly towards her. She said unsteadily, 'I . . . I cannot wear this. It shows my shape!'

'Indeed it does—most entrancingly.' There was a glint in his eyes. 'When my mother was a girl, the more daring young ladies used to dampen the muslin so that it would cling even more closely to their bodies. But, for the sake of modesty, you will wear a silk underskirt tomorrow which also belonged to my mother. Alice is airing it for you.'

'The gown does not fit me,' Emerald began desperately.

'Nonsense!' He touched the neckline. 'It might have been made for you.'

She passed her tongue over suddenly dry lips. His fingers, pretending to adjust the neckline of the gown, seemed to burn into her flesh. He bent his head without warning, and his mouth was at the base of her throat, kissing the soft flesh, while his hands moved caressingly over her body. She tried to move away, but the blood was thundering in her veins, and when he lifted his head and their lips met, her mouth parted under his.

If his kiss had reminded her of Andrew's, she might have taken comfort from it and surrendered herself to a moment of self-delusion. But this was not remotely how Andrew had ever kissed her. This was a totally demoralising experience, sapping her will and her strength, carrying her along on a torrent of passion which she knew would overwhelm her unless she fought it with everything at her command.

He was not in the least put out when her frantic struggles forced him to release her. '*Tomorrow*,' he said, a bright glitter in his eyes, and moved to the door.

Emerald's supper tray was brought in to her, and then removed again, barely touched. She lay in bed afterwards, unable to sleep, jangled emotions conflicting inside her.

Judah could not have made it more abundantly plain that he expected more than a platonic marriage of convenience. As for herself—she did not love him, did not even like him. He was a hard, vindictive, man who did not scruple to remind her, whenever it suited him, that he had virtually bought her for twenty sovereigns. With utter ruthlessness, he had forced her to accompany him to Coorabee Creek, deliberately keeping her in ignorance so that she would discover the truth about Andrew in the most shocking manner. Even if her love did not belong irrevocably to Andrew, how could she ever feel anything but hatred for Judah Renshaw? And yet . . .

And yet, how was she ever going to win the fight to keep their marriage on a platonic plane when his slightest touch made her feel so devastated and abandoned and *alive*?

She was heavy-eyed with lack of sleep when her wedding day dawned. A pale but otherwise composed Alice entered with the silk underskirt which Emerald was to wear beneath the muslin gown, and also a bonnet trimmed with ruched white silk and blue cornflowers.

Emerald breakfasted in her room, and then left to join Judah. He looked unfamiliar and imposing in well-cut trousers, a silk shirt with flowing cravat and a tail-coat. He said nothing as he took her arm and led her outside to where Murphy was waiting to drive them to the courthouse. Both of them were preoccupied with their own thoughts during the journey.

The township in which the courthouse was located boasted no more than half a dozen buildings of various types, scattered haphazardly and with no sense of coherence or design. Emerald glimpsed the general store, with its rows of animal skins hanging up outside, and Judah pointed out to her the house where the magistrate resided. The courthouse itself was a crude construction with a lock-up cell at the rear for the confinement of prisoners.

The wedding ceremony was attended by numerous ill-assorted individuals who just happened to be in the township and who wandered inside the courthouse to witness the proceedings. Since they were all men, Emerald's outmoded gown drew nothing but admiring glances from them. With the minimum of ritual, Judah and Emerald were pronounced man and wife.

A strange sense of unreality gripped Emerald as they started the return journey. Judah broke the silence.

'I'm afraid the men who were in the courthouse will go home and fetch their wives before descending on us. A celebration will be expected. I shall have to dole out rum rations to all my workers, and you will have to be presented to everyone.'

'I understand,' Emerald began, and stopped as the clatter of hooves reached them from behind. Then they were almost forced off the track as a horseman overtook them and reined in ahead of them. Murphy soothed and controlled their horses and halted too.

With bemusement and a racing heart Emerald saw Andrew swinging himself from the saddle and moving towards them. He ignored Judah completely, and addressed her.

'I was on my way to explain matters to you,' he said, 'and to ask you to forgive me and marry me.'

She stared at him, the blood draining from her face. But before she could utter a sound, Judah said with harsh mockery, 'You're too late, my friend!'

Emerald found her voice. '*Marry* you,' she echoed. 'But . . . you are already married!'

Andrew's face darkened with a complex mixture of emotions which she was far too confused to define. 'No, I am not. Surely Judah Renshaw must have told you the whole story by now?'

She turned slowly to face Judah. Whatever the 'whole story' was, he had deliberately allowed her to go on believing that Andrew was married and out of her reach.

She was speechless, too shattered even for anger. She had known that Judah was ruthless and treacherous, but she had never even guessed at the lengths to which he was prepared to go in order to get what he wanted.

CHAPTER FOUR

Before Emerald could recover sufficiently to react at all, Judah addressed Andrew with a note of malevolent triumph in his voice. 'We are just returning from the courthouse, where we were legally and irrevocably wed. You are not only too late, but you are also blocking our way!'

'Married . . .' Andrew echoed incredulously, staring at Emerald.

'Out of the way!' Judah snapped, and commanded the driver, 'Whip up the horses, Murphy!'

Andrew was forced to throw himself clear. His own horse whickered and then bolted, and when Emerald turned round in her seat she saw Andrew running to catch it.

Everything—the shock of discovering too late that Andrew was not married after all, the realisation that Judah had deliberately kept that knowledge from her, and now his arrogant and brutal refusal to allow Andrew the explanations which were due to her—crystallised in Emerald's brain. She turned on Judah in blind rage, her fingers curled to claw at his face.

'You *fiend!*' she ground out. 'Oh, you treacherous, despicable cur . . .'

Her hands were imprisoned in a hard hold,

rendering them impotent. 'Be quiet!' he commanded.

'I shall not be quiet!' she shouted at him, struggling to free her hands. 'You knew—you knew all the time . . . And yet you allowed me to go on believing that . . .'

'Emerald,' Judah said with ominous calm. 'I told you to be quiet. I do not launder dirty linen in public.' He released her, and clapped a hand on Murphy's shoulder.

'If I find out that you have repeated a single syllable of what you have heard to a soul,' he warned the overseer, 'you'll never work for me or anyone else in this part of the interior again!'

'*Me*, sor?' the Irishman returned in an injured voice. 'Why, sure, and whyever would I go blabbin' when I didn't hear a t'ing?'

'Good!' Judah settled back, and addressed Emerald in a menacing whisper. 'You would do well to remember, my dear, that I do not suffer being abused, either verbally or physically, in front of the servants.'

She glared at him in reply, and the journey continued in grim, tense silence.

Emerald's helpless rage was temporarily banked down as other thoughts began to pound in her brain like rats caught in a treadmill. Andrew wasn't married. Who, then, was the pretty fair-haired woman who had worn a wedding ring and called him 'darling'? She could hardly have been another convict servant. And if Andrew hadn't appeased his father by marrying a suitable young lady with a dowry, where had the money come from to pay for that well-set-up farmstead and the house with its liveried servants?

Then, once more, the outrageous thought began to hammer in her mind, gathering a renewed momentum of fury—*Judah Renshaw had deliberately and inexcusably tricked her into marrying him.*

When they reached the house she refused, rigid with rage, the hand which he held out to help her from the wagonette. As they climbed the steps to the veranda, Alice met them, pale but composed.

'May I be the first to wish you happiness, Mr and Mrs Renshaw,' she began.

Emerald uttered an angry, bitter laugh which was cut off abruptly when Judah dug his fingers with painful warning into the flesh of her arm. He answered Alice formally.

'On behalf of my wife and myself, thank you, Alice. Now, you'd better warn Hettie and the girls to get busy in the kitchen, preparing food. We'll soon be invaded by self-invited guests.'

'Very well, sir.'

Still holding Emerald's arm, he led her along the veranda to the room where he did his accounts and kept his guns.

'Let us establish one thing,' he told her, his voice hard. 'In public, whatever your private feelings may be, you will conduct yourself as a dutiful wife should!'

She drew a gasping breath of outrage. 'How dare *you* censure *me*? After everything you have done! When I leapt to the conclusion that Andrew had married someone else, you deliberately allowed me to go on believing it!'

'You would scarcely have found the truth more palatable,' he assured her grimly.

Her anger momentarily pushed aside, she formed the questions which had been churning in her brain. 'What *is* the truth, Judah? Who is the fair-haired woman who lives in Andrew's house, and whom I assumed to be his wife?'

'*His* house!' Judah echoed with a crack of sour laughter. 'It is my brother Saul's house. Andrew Standish manages my brother's share of Coorabee Creek.'

Emerald stared at him, dumbfounded. Andrew had always given the impression, in his letters, that he farmed his own grant of land. 'The . . . the woman I saw with him . . .' she began.

'Is Saul's wife, my sister-in-law Claire.' Judah's voice had turned hard as flint. 'Saul is a helpless cripple, and Standish not only runs the property as he chooses but also shares Claire's bed. That fact must have been very clear to you when you ran from the house in the way you did—even though you supposed them to be married.'

Completely overwhelmed, Emerald sank weakly into a chair. 'How . . . how did it all come about?' she managed, after a while.

A look of revulsion crossed Judah's face. 'It sickens me to talk about it. You'll learn the whole sordid story soon enough from others. It's the talk of the district.' He moved to the door. 'Now, if you will excuse me, I have to dole out rum rations to the convicts in celebration of our marriage.'

He left her there and went outside, and she sat with her head sunk in her hands. *Andrew*, her heart mourned. *How could he have changed so radically, become so corrupt?*

Her very soul seemed to shrivel with humiliation as she imagined the interview which must have taken place between him and Claire before he came, too late, to ask Emerald to marry him.

'If you made her your wife,' his mistress would have argued, *'tongues would cease to wag, and nothing will really change between us, darling. She will just have to put up with the situation . . .'*

Her bitter thoughts were interrupted when Alice knocked on the door, and said quietly, 'The first guests will soon be arriving, Mrs Renshaw. Hettie is setting out a buffet meal in the main front room. Perhaps you ought to check that everything is to your satisfaction.'

Emerald sighed. 'I'm sure it will be. Has Murphy collected my carpet-bags yet? The women will be outraged by this gown.'

'I think Mr Renshaw must have forgotten to order him to do so. Murphy has left with a keg of rum to be distributed among the farm constables and shared out between the other convicts.' She smiled faintly at Emerald. 'The gown becomes you, madam, and the other women will assume that it is the latest London fashion.'

Emerald shrugged. Compared with the fact that her entire life lay in ruins, what did it matter what impression she made?

As she followed Alice from the room, she remarked, 'You spoke of farm constables. Surely you don't mean dragoons?'

'No, madam. It is a term used for ex-convicts who are appointed to control the labour force still serving their sentences.'

Momentarily forgetting that Alice was, herself, a convict, Emerald said, 'There must be a vast army of felons on the property to merit a full keg of rum . . .'

'Indeed, madam. On a large station such as this the convicts are scattered and accommodated in huts near where they are working. The ones who have been lining up outside the house for their rum rations are the home-station convicts. The rest are seldom seen by anyone but Murphy, who supervises the farm constables and makes regular inspections, and delivers the food rations once a week.'

Emerald spared a moment's compassion for that unseen army of felons which laboured on Coorabee Creek and lived in scattered huts, and then her own problems claimed her attention again.

The self-invited guests were arriving, and continued to arrive throughout the afternoon. Hettie's buffet lunch became a feast which extended to high tea, and showed all signs of expanding into supper.

The majority of the guests were weather-beaten farmers with equally weather-beaten wives. At Emerald's request, Alice had lent her a fringed shawl to wear which served to subdue the outrageously immodest muslin gown, and the women merely accepted the whole *ensemble* as some new English fashion, outlandish and no doubt considered smart, but not for the likes of them.

As Judah had predicted, it was not long before Emerald began to learn about the scandal created by his sister-in-law Claire and Andrew.

'I understand that you know Mr Standish's family in England,' one of the women said to Emerald. 'Will you be writing to tell them about the situation in which he finds himself?'

'That will depend,' Emerald replied deliberately, 'on whether or not I can successfully sift out the truth from the gossip.'

An eager circle of women surrounded her, avid to share details of the scandal with the newcomer.

'It all started, you see, Mrs Renshaw, after Judah's sister Mary and her husband were killed in the Aboriginal attack. Saul and Judah hurried to help as soon as they received news of what was happening, but they arrived too late. The house was already ablaze, and the Aborigines were breaking into the store where the rum was kept . . .'

'And in the fighting which followed,' someone else took up the story, 'Saul was struck in the spine by an axe. His life hung in the balance for a long time, and even though he recovered, he is now a bed-bound cripple, little more than a vegetable. So when young Andrew Standish arrived soon afterwards, looking for work as a station manager, Judah and Claire welcomed him with open arms!'

'I believe Claire's arms were wide open, even then, for quite a different reason,' one of the women put in cynically. 'She must have realised that Saul would never be a husband to her again, even if he lived.'

'Well, *I* place most of the blame on Standish,' another argued. 'After all, if Saul had died, and young Standish had married Claire, he would have gained ownership of a sizeable piece of Coorabee Creek!'

'Does Saul have any inkling of what is going on?' Emerald asked.

'Indeed not! Since he cannot leave his bed, he is all too easy to fool, and no one visiting him would be cruel enough even to hint at the situation.'

'And of course, the convict servant who caught them together in the first place was immediately packed off to another station . . .'

Sickened, Emerald deliberately changed the

conversation, only to find it brought back to the subject of convict servants in general.

'The only way to get them to do anything,' a stout matron declared, 'is to have them flogged again and again until their spirits have been broken.'

'But how dreadful!' Emerald exclaimed.

'Yes, indeed, my dear. They *are* a dreadful set of felons.'

'I did not mean that! I find it abominable that fellow human beings should be physically abused until they have been cowed into submission like animals!'

The women exchanged patronising smiles. 'You'll learn, my dear.'

Flushing with a sense of outrage which none of them would have understood, she excused herself and went to find Judah, who was talking to the men at the far end of the room. She drew him aside, and said in low tones,

'I can understand, now, why you hate Andrew. And indeed, I shall never forgive him for what he has done to me. At the same time, I cannot forgive what *you* did. You used my mistake in order to trick me into marrying you.'

'That's right,' he admitted coolly. 'I saw my opportunity, and I took it. You were crushed and beaten when you ran from Saul's house. I did not want to give you the chance to recover, to whip up that temper of yours and return to demand your fare home from Standish.'

'You really are a devil,' Emerald said helplessly. 'I would willingly have stayed on as unpaid governess to the children until you could replace me with another, willing bride bid for at a Sydney auction. Why did you have to *marry* me?'

'I wanted you,' he said simply.

She looked at him, and their eyes locked. She was the first to glance away. 'Talking of the children,' she said unevenly. 'I . . . I think I ought to look in on them. Please—apologise for my temporary disappearance . . .'

She made her escape, her mind in a turmoil. If only it were possible to turn back the hands of the clock; if only she had not allowed herself to be lured to this alien colony by Andrew's lying letters of love, only to find herself trapped in marriage with a man who was unscrupulous and arrogant and profoundly disturbing.

She arrived at the children's bedroom just as Alice was leaving it. 'They have behaved remarkably well this afternoon, madam,' Alice reported. 'I had feared they would burst in upon the adults, and demand that Mr Renshaw should see them into bed.'

'It is understandable that they should cling to him,' Emerald said. 'I must strive to gain their affection and their confidence.'

After all, she reflected bleakly, *it was what I had been bought for in the first place.*

But when she entered the children's room, and said brightly, 'I've come to kiss you goodnight,' Timothy pointedly turned his face to the wall.

'I don't want to be kissed,' he muttered. 'Selina doesn't want to be kissed either.'

'I see. Well, perhaps tomorrow night you would like me to tell you a bed-time story?'

'I do not like stories,' Timothy interrupted, adding predictably, 'Selina does not like stories either.'

There was nothing for it but to admit temporary

defeat. Emerald bade them goodnight and returned to the guests.

Those who had travelled long distances appeared, as a matter of course, to expect to stay the night, and this seemed to be the accepted way of things, for Alice came in to ask how many extra bedrooms needed to be prepared.

When all the guests had said goodnight, Emerald headed gratefully for the lilac room. Suddenly Judah was by her side, his hand on her arm.

'Where do you think you are going?'

'I am going to bed.'

'Not in here! You'd certainly give the Camerons something to talk about if you were to burst in, expecting to spend the night! I told Alice to put them in the lilac room.' His eyes glinted at her. 'There is only one spare sleeping-space in this house tonight, and that is in my bed!'

Before she could stop him or protest, he had scooped her into his arms and was walking with her towards the main bedroom which Alice had earlier pointed out to her. To have made a fuss would have brought their guests running, so Emerald, seething, forced herself to remain silent until he had set her down and closed the bedroom door behind him.

His eyes held hers in a challenge. 'Well, my reluctant little bride?'

'If you imagine for one moment . . .' she began through clenched teeth.

She was silenced by his mouth upon hers, tantalising and seductively probing. He made no move to touch her in any other way and she could easily have jerked her head away had she wanted to. But a strange weakness had crept over her, and almost without realising what she was doing she moved towards him. Only then did his arms enclose her, drawing her against him.

In that flimsy, outmoded muslin gown which had been fashioned during a less inhibited era, she was intensely aware of the masculine body pressed against hers. Whenever Andrew had embraced her in the past there had been yards of stiff material, stays and petticoats separating them physically, so that she was experiencing demoralising sensations for the first time.

And yet they were also curiously familiar sensations, as though she had always known intuitively that *this* was what it would be like, and that her senses would be inflamed to the extent where she would no longer be capable of offering resistance.

Judah's hands moved down her hips, caressing their contours, moulding her body to his and lifting her up so that their thighs met. A small, sane, corner of her mind told her that if she did not fight back now, she would be for ever lost. She would have allowed him to take possession of her—a man she did not love, a man who had tricked her into marrying him at a time when she was as vulnerable as any woman could possibly be. A man, moreover, who had regarded her from the beginning as a commodity for which he had paid good money.

She pushed at his chest, but his kiss became more insistent, his embrace an insidious and skilled tactic designed to bring her to surrender. She was no match for him physically, and neither could she fight the demoralising power he had over her senses. And they both knew it.

He lifted his mouth from hers, still holding her

close, and smiled into her eyes. 'No longer quite so reluctant, are you?' he whispered, gently taunting. 'Shall we go to bed?'

She chose her words with chilling care, knowing that words were the only weapons she possessed with which to fight against the effect he had upon her.

'You've bought me, Judah Renshaw. I belong to you in the same way as your livestock does. So let us go to bed, and I'll suffer you to take whatever you think twenty sovereigns entitles you to. Afterwards, I shall consider any debt I owe you in that direction to have been settled in full.'

He released her as suddenly as if the touch of her had scorched him. His face was stark, the expression in his eyes quite frightening for a moment.

'I have never,' he said, biting off the words, 'needed to force a woman against her will, or had her *suffer* my attentions!'

'Then it will be an entirely new experience for you, won't it!'

He uttered an oath under his breath. 'Thank you, no! The next move will come from you, or not at all!'

Instead of experiencing the sense of victory she had expected, she felt curiously flat. But she hid her reaction by saying with studied indifference, 'In that case, I take it that you intend moving back to Alice's bed, and leaving me in occupation here. And, once our guests have departed, I shall return to the lilac room.'

'Oh, no,' he interrupted grimly. 'If I choose to share any other woman's bed it will be entirely my own concern. But tonight, with the house full of guests, I'll not run any risk of starting a scandal. As for your returning to the lilac room, there'll be no question of that.'

'But . . .'

He gave a hard, mirthless laugh. 'We might as well begin in the manner in which I intend that we shall be going on. We'll share this room.'

With a trapped expression, Emerald regarded the capacious four-poster which dominated the room. It was large enough, certainly, to accommodate two people without forcing them to touch if they did not wish to. But sharing it with Judah promised to be a challenge which she did not feel herself equipped to meet.

He had obviously misinterpreted what was in her mind, for he went on with a sour grin, 'You will have the bed, and I shall sleep in the dressing-room on the sofa.'

She cast a glance in the direction he had indicated, and noticed for the first time that a doorless cubicle led from it and held a long mirror, a bureau and a sofa. Such an arrangement would afford no privacy for either of them.

'It will have to do for tonight,' she said. 'But I don't see why I should not return to the lilac room tomorrow night . . .'

'Because,' he interrupted, 'I have no intention of having the household—and therefore the whole of the interior—knowing that you don't share my bed!'

He added with acid humour, 'You need not be concerned about the close proximity of our sleeping quarters. You'll be more than safe from my attentions, I assure you. Now I'll go and take a turn on the veranda while you're preparing for bed.'

Emerald discovered that Murphy had returned to pick up her carpet-bags some time during the afternoon, and that Alice had unpacked for her. She washed and dressed hastily for bed, and snuffed out the candles before curling up in the huge four-poster. Judah could undress in the dark. She had found a chenille coverlet in a bureau drawer and had placed it on the sofa for his use.

Instinct told her that he had meant what he'd said. He would not force his attentions on her. She wondered why she did not feel triumphant or even comforted by the thought..

It had been a long day, a day in which her spirits had been battered by one event after another, one devastating discovery after another. She shed a few bitter tears for Andrew's treachery and for the death of a dream, and then sleep overcame her. She did not stir when Judah returned to the room.

When she awoke in the morning he had already risen and left. For the benefit of their guests he played an attentive, devoted role during breakfast, telling her that he meant to select a safe mount for her so that she could learn to ride.

'It is essential in the interior, my dear, that one should know how to handle a horse.'

'Thank you,' Emerald murmured. 'I should very much like to learn.'

As soon as their guests had departed, his manner became one of formal politeness, and that night he waited, once again, until Emerald was asleep before he retired. When she awoke, he was gone.

That became the set pattern of their marriage. Or—was that really how it was? The suspicion sidled into Emerald's mind, and she was astonished to discover how very unwelcome—how almost enraging—it was.

Did he in reality spend his nights with Alice?

There was never any visible sign in the mornings that the sofa had been occupied at all. The matching cushion was always plumped up, the chenille coverlet neatly folded and placed inside the wardrobe.

Emerald became obsessed with her suspicions, and one night she determined to remain awake until morning if she had to.

The clock in the parlour had just struck midnight when she heard Judah entering the room. A mixture of feelings which she could not, or did not, care to identify flooded her. But she kept her eyes closed, and waited for him to move into the dressing-room. Instead, light from the candle he was holding struck her closed eyelids, and she realised with a pounding heart that he had stopped by her bed and was looking down at her. She forced herself to breathe evenly, as though fast asleep.

She almost betrayed herself when she felt the warmth of his fingers against her brow. He was smoothing away a lock of hair; it was the merest touch and if she had truly been asleep she would have been utterly unaware of it. She heard him utter a muffled oath. Then the flickering light was no longer striking her closed eyelids, and she caught the very slight sounds he made as he moved into his allotted domain.

Emerald smiled to herself. Not only was he *not* spending his nights with Alice; he was taking great pains to prevent anyone in the house from guessing that he occupied the dressing-room, and that was why it was always so immaculate when he left it each morning. Something very like tenderness filled her at the thought.

She often wondered, later, how their relationship might have altered at that stage if something completely outside her control had not happened during the early hours of the morning. She was awakened from a deep sleep by Judah shaking her shoulder.

'What . . . ?' she began in confusion. She could only see his face dimly in the dark.

'You were weeping in your sleep,' he said curtly, 'and calling Standish's name.'

She could not even recall the dream, and only now did she become aware that her cheeks were wet with tears. 'I'm—sorry I disturbed you,' she muttered.

He made no response, but returned to his own bed on the sofa. And after breakfast, later, he announced abruptly that he was leaving immediately for Port Phillip, where he had business to conduct, and that he would be away for an indefinite period.

The days were long and strangely bleak without him. Emerald performed a sad and secret little ritual of burning Andrew's letters, and tried to fill the emptiness in her life by learning to ride, and by trying to gain the children's confidence—which was proving to be an unequal struggle.

From Alice, she learnt that Coorabee Creek was one enormous farmstead comprising many thousands of acres.

'Mr Renshaw's grandfather,' Alice said, 'came to New South Wales as a free settler, and he chose to take up his grant of land here at the foothills of the Blue Mountains. As his family increased, the old gentleman took up more land surrounding him, until the station grew to its present size. But now the only Renshaws left are Mr Saul and Mr Judah—and of course, Miss Mary's children.'

If Emerald had needed proof that Alice had once been Judah's mistress, this intimate knowledge of the family history supplied it. She was astonished by the stab of resentment which pierced her.

Intuitively, Alice must have known what was passing through her mind, for she flushed and said, 'Madam—I want you to understand about Mr Renshaw and me. We were hurting no one. He never pretended that he loved me, and as soon as the children came to live here he ended what had been between us. I cannot pretend that it didn't grieve me, but I shall never regret what we had. He made me realise, for the first time in my life, that it is possible for a man to be gentle and caring and compassionate.'

A violent mixture of feelings seized Emerald. She did not recognise the Judah Alice had been describing, and for some unaccountable reason she felt cheated. She looked away and said colourlessly,

'I understand.'

'I don't believe you do, madam, with respect,' Alice corrected in a quiet voice. 'My father was a brutal man, and so was my husband. But for Mr Renshaw I would probably have drifted into marriage with yet another brutal man after I had worked my ticket. As it is, I have learnt to discriminate, and I look forward with confidence to the future after I receive my freedom. So please do not begrudge me what there once was between us.'

'I don't,' Emerald responded, making her voice

as neutral as she could. But inside she was seething with rage. What did she care about Judah's former relationship with Alice? He was probably, at this very moment, being *gentle and caring and compassionate* towards some other female in Port Phillip, while the wife he had tricked into unwilling marriage was left kicking her heels in boredom and frustration . . .

She swallowed hard, and determinedly changed the subject. 'Look at those children! They spurn all my efforts to amuse and entertain them, and what better do they find to do?'

Alice glanced up from her sewing at the two children who were moodily sitting on the bottom step of the veranda and scratching with sticks in the sandy soil.

'I know how hard you have been trying to get close to the children, madam. A thought has occurred to me which might be of help. It will be Selina's birthday soon, so if you were to purchase a gift for her from the store—Mr Renshaw has an account there.'

'I shall do more than that!' Emerald said on a sudden inspiration, and rose. 'Thank you for the suggestion, Alice!'

She descended the veranda steps, cheerfully inviting the children to make room for her beside them.

Instead, Timothy stood up, forcing his young sister to do the same, and they faced Emerald with their usual guarded expressions.

'I hear it will soon be Selina's birthday,' she said, refusing to be discouraged. 'How would you two like to visit the store with me tomorrow and select some special treats with which to mark the day?'

'Oh yes, pl—' Selina began eagerly, but stopped when her brother nudged her sharply.

'How would we travel to the store?' Timothy wanted to know.

'Why, in the wagonette, driven by Murphy.'

'I don't like Murphy,' Timothy stated flatly. 'Selina doesn't like Murphy either. We'd like to go if *you* would drive us—Aunt Emerald.'

It was the first time the child had ever addressed her by any title. That, coupled with the fact that he wished her to drive them, gave Emerald hope. But she said regretfully, 'I fear I'm not competent to handle the wagonette.'

'We could take the pony and trap,' Timothy pointed out. 'Even *I* could drive the pony and trap.'

'It would be too long a journey for a pony.'

'No, it wouldn't. There is a stream where it could be watered and rested along the way.'

'Very well,' Emerald gave in.

The beginning of a smile touched Timothy's lips. 'What kind of special treat may we choose, Aunt Emerald?'

'Why—anything within reason.'

The children looked at one another, and then nodded, and Emerald felt that she had taken a significant step forward in establishing a relationship with them.

They set off in the pony and trap early the next morning. Emerald had allowed Timothy to take the reins, and the doughty pony trotted briskly along the track which led from the house towards the township. They had reached a fork in the track when Timothy reined in, and turned to Emerald.

'Selina and me have chosen the special treat we want. We don't want anything from the store.

Selina and me want to go and visit Auntie Claire.'

As the truth dawned on her, Emerald mentally cursed herself for a fool. The children—or rather Timothy—had cleverly manoeuvred her into this position. He hadn't wanted Murphy to drive them, for he had known—by the instinct for such knowledge which all children possess—that his Auntie Claire's house was out of bounds to them, and that Murphy would have refused to take them there.

'I . . .' she began. 'The agreement was to go to the store, Timothy.'

'You said anything within reason,' he reminded her doggedly.

'Yes, but . . .'

'*Why* can't we visit Auntie Claire?' he challenged. 'Uncle Judah won't say.'

Emerald bit her lip. *Because your Auntie Claire is living in adultery,* she thought. *Because Judah naturally does not want you to associate with the woman who is cuckolding his crippled brother. And because I cannot bear to face either her or Andrew, and exacerbate wounds which have not even started to heal yet . . .*

But she could not explain any of this to the children, and in the meantime they were looking at her with a mixture of challenge, and hope, and a resigned suspicion that she would deny them the one thing they wanted.

At last Emerald said, 'Very well. We'll visit your Auntie Claire.'

She would have to grit her teeth and bear it, and hope that Judah never learnt of the visit. It was her only chance of establishing a bond between herself and the children.

Her mouth was dry and her heart was beating

stormily by the time they arrived at the house. The children scrambled from the trap, shouting, 'Auntie Claire! Auntie Claire!' as they ran to the veranda. This was the first time Emerald had ever seen them behaving like normal, happy children.

She followed them on leaden feet, after handing over the pony to a hovering servant. When she reached the veranda, the pretty fair-haired woman was kneeling down, each child clasped in her arms, her smiling face streaked with tears as she hugged and kissed them in turn.

Claire Renshaw rose when Emerald appeared, and gave the children a gentle push towards the door. 'Go and ask Maria for buttermilk and biscuits.'

Watching the children run inside the house, Emerald exclaimed involuntarily, 'How stupid of me! Of course, they must have lived with you after their parents were killed! And they have been pining for you!'

'Yes,' Claire Renshaw said simply. 'Judah took them away from me, after . . .' She stopped, and looked at Emerald, and went on with quiet dignity, 'I am glad to meet you at last. I have wanted, so much, to tell you how very sorry I am about everything. I would not blame you for hating me.'

Far from hating her, Emerald was surprised to realise that, under different circumstances, she and Claire could have become friends.

'If it makes it any easier for you to bear,' she heard Claire go on, 'the—situation—between Andrew and myself lasted for only a short while, although no one in the district would ever believe that . . .'

'Please,' Emerald cut her short. 'I'd rather not talk about it. And I should prefer not to have to face Andrew.'

'There is no fear of that. He is out, organising the annual mustering of the cattle.' She placed a tentative hand on Emerald's arm. 'I . . . should like to thank you very much for having defied Judah, and for bringing the children to see me.'

'I have not precisely defied him. The children themselves trapped me into bringing them. But now that they have, I am glad.' She smiled at Claire. 'And since I don't wish to intrude on your reunion with them, I shall just sit quietly on the veranda, if I may, until it is time for us to return.'

'You are very understanding. My time with the children will be most precious, for I don't expect this visit to be repeated. But you will certainly not be left to sit alone on the veranda! My husband would be delighted to meet you, and I shall have refreshments sent to his room.'

'I would very much like to meet Judah's brother,' Emerald said.

'Then please follow me.'

In this house, too, the bedrooms led directly off the veranda, and Saul Renshaw's room was situated at the far end of the one on the left side, where a large tree cast its shade over it.

Emerald hovered in the background while Claire opened the door, and announced, 'Dearest, I have brought the most delightful visitor to see you! And there is another treat in store for you later!' She turned to Emerald, and mouthed conspiratorially, 'Don't mention that you have brought the children.'

Emerald merely nodded. Claire Renshaw's devotion to her husband seemed total and genuine. Things did not add up.

Then Emerald was being ushered into the room where a powerfully-built man lay in bed. Physically, he was an older version of Judah. But his face bore the legacy of physical pain, and his eyes were wise and kind and tolerant, whereas Judah's usually sparked with passion of one kind or another, or else surveyed the world cynically.

Claire introduced them, and then withdrew. Emerald sat down beside the bed. 'I am so very pleased to meet you . . .' she began.

'And I you. First of all, I have to beg your forgiveness for the very great wrong I have done you.'

Emerald frowned in bewilderment. 'What possible wrong could *you* have done me?'

Saul Renshaw sighed. 'Not only you, my dear. You see, I am responsible for everything that has happened—for the scandal which has engulfed my poor wife, for your rushing into marriage with my brother.'

'I don't understand . . .'

'It was I,' he said in a quiet voice, 'who deliberately, in the full knowledge of what I was doing, pushed my dearest Claire and your Andrew into one another's arms. I planned that they should become lovers. I did not want my wife to face long, empty years without tenderness or comfort.'

CHAPTER FIVE

EMERALD STARED at Saul Renshaw. 'I'm sorry, but—I find it impossible to believe. If you loved your wife . . .'

'It was *because* I loved her that I acted as I did.' Saul heaved a sigh. 'I am a cripple, my dear. I shall always be a cripple, helplessly trapped in my bed for the rest of my life. I shall never be a husband to Claire again in anything but name. And she is a young woman, in the full bloom of her beauty. I loved her too much to want to condemn her to sharing my own lonely road.'

'I see,' Emerald said quietly. 'You are a most generous and selfless man.'

He gave her a wry smile. 'Not quite as selfless as you imagine. Andrew was a gentleman and an equal, quite unlike most of the men out here who offer themselves as managers. I wanted him to become part of our lives. What I had in mind was a permanent—if unorthodox—arrangement which would offer an acceptable compromise to all three of us.'

'Nevertheless,' Emerald said, 'I cannot see Judah, for instance, viewing matters in the same light if he were to find himself in your situation.'

'No, indeed. Judah is far too passionately possessive, too unwilling to compromise.' Saul smiled faintly. 'I sometimes feel that if Judah had been crippled instead, he would have overcome his handicap by sheer will-power. He would have forced his useless spine to support his body or died in the attempt. But we are not all of us made the same.'

Emerald was silent for a while. Then she said, 'Judah blames Andrew and Claire. Don't you feel that you owe it to both of them to tell your brother the truth?'

'My dear girl, I tried. When Judah found out what was going on, he arrived here like an avenging fury. He found Andrew in the stockyard, and I learnt later that he had had to be forcibly restrained from killing Andrew. Then my brother came to see me and tried to pretend that he'd had a dispute with Andrew about cattle straying into his sheep pastures. I told him the truth—that I knew about the scandal which had erupted, that I had instigated the affair. He flatly refused to believe me.'

'Yes, I suppose I can understand that. It *is* difficult to believe . . .'

'More so for Judah than for anyone else. You see, my younger brother has always tended to hero-worship me, and invest me with far more virtues than I really possess. When I told him the literal truth he convinced himself that I was trying to shoulder Claire's guilt, and therefore Andrew's as well.'

Saul added wryly, 'To be fair, he had a valid point. I *would* have shouldered Claire's guilt if she really had betrayed me, and Judah knows this. I'm afraid he will never believe that the blame is mine. He decided to protect me from further hurt by putting it about that I know nothing of the affair, and he threatened the most dire consequences to anyone who dared mention it to me. So there the matter rests, with Andrew and Claire the villains of the piece, and I would only make matters worse if I were to declare publicly that I not only knew about it but that I had engineered it.'

'Yes,' Emerald was forced to admit. 'It really would fan the flames of the scandal.'

'And all my scheming and my plotting were in vain,' Saul went on softly. 'What was between Claire and Andrew was swiftly over and meant nothing. My beautiful wife wanted only me.'

Emerald's thoughts were spinning, but even so she could not help registering the look of pride and self-esteem in Saul's eyes. If he had once seen himself as no more than a crippled liability to Claire, he no longer did so. He had regained stature in his own view.

She was spared the necessity of thinking of something suitable to say, for they were interrupted by a servant carrying a tray of tea. Emerald eyed the tray uncertainly, wondering whether Saul could drink his unaided or whether she ought to offer to help him. But then Claire entered the room with the children, and after she had poured two cups of tea and handed one to Emerald, she propped pillows behind her husband's head and casually offered him his cup. He was, it appeared, paralysed only from the waist down.

The children's conversation lent an air of domesticity to the scene. They competed with one another to tell their uncle all their news; small items of information which were obviously important to them, but which they had withheld from both Alice and Emerald.

'Selina lost a tooth . . .' Timothy began.

'It was *my* tooth, Timothy, so *I* want to tell about it! Uncle Saul, it was all wobbly when I pushed it with my tongue.'

'There wasn't any blood when it came out,' her brother said disparagingly.

'There *was*, Timothy! Auntie Claire, make him stop telling about my tooth!'

Claire restored peace, and Emerald watched and listened to them in silence. One thing was becoming very clear to her. These two children had gone to live with Claire and Saul immediately after their own parents were killed. They had forged emotional bonds with the couple during an intensely traumatic time, and there was little chance of the children transferring those bonds to Emerald, no matter how hard she might try.

When they had finished their tea, Claire suggested that Emerald might like to see the rest of the house. It was an obvious manoeuvre to allow Saul to enjoy the children's undivided attention.

As the two women went from room to room, Claire explained, 'This was the site of the original homestead, built by Saul's grandfather, and later extended and then completely rebuilt. When Saul's father died, Coorabee Creek was split into three equal parts, and Judah and Mary's husband built homes of their own on their shares of the property . . .'

Claire's voice tailed off under Emerald's intent gaze. 'I don't suppose you want to talk about Coorabee Creek's history,' she added with a faint smile.

'No,' Emerald agreed quietly. 'Your husband

has told me the truth about you and Andrew. I don't blame you, but Andrew... *Did I really mean so very little to him?*' she finished in bleak, tormented tones.

'Don't judge him too harshly,' Claire pleaded. 'Try to understand. Andrew came into our lives at a time when he needed us almost as much as we needed him.'

'I *don't* understand!' Emerald cried, thinking only of her own pain and loss.

Claire placed a hand on her arm. 'Andrew came to us, a beaten man. His life at Wallalong had been incredibly hard and dogged by failure. He was forced to give up his grant of land and seek work with someone else as an ordinary stockman. The offer of a post as manager here was a godsend to him.'

'He lied to me in his letters,' Emerald said bitterly. 'He gave the impression that he was working for himself on a more congenial grant of land. He made Coorabee Creek sound like the name of a district, and not one vast farm station of which he merely managed a third share!'

'I dare say he did not want to admit to you that he had failed. It was that failure which made him vulnerable and in need of comfort—just as I was in need of comfort.'

Her hand tightened on Emerald's arm. 'That was all it ever was—the mutual giving and receiving of comfort. Andrew never stopped loving you, any more than I ever stopped loving Saul. Even if we hadn't been found together one night by one of the convict servants, so that the scandal broke, it would have lasted only for a short time.'

Emerald broke away from her and fled blindly,

descending the veranda steps, her arms hugged to her breast.

Fool, fool! her mind cried wildly. *Why could you not have waited until you knew the whole truth, instead of allowing Judah to trick you into a mockery of a marriage?*

She became aware that Claire had joined her, and struggled for some degree of composure. She voiced the first thought which entered her head. 'The garden is beautiful. I had not expected to find cultivated flowers out here.'

Keeping the conversation upon mundane matters, Claire replied, 'I brought many of the seeds with me from England, after I'd married Saul. They do well here because of the tributary of the Murrumbidgee River which runs close to the house. Listen—can you hear it?'

Obediently, mechanically, Emerald tilted her head and caught the sound of water rippling over stones.

'It has never been known to dry up,' Claire went on. 'Not even in the severest drought, so that we have no problems regarding irrigation.'

Emerald changed the subject abruptly. 'We'd better leave now, or Alice will send out search-parties for us.'

Claire made a sad gesture of resignation. 'I understand. Thank you once more for having brought the children. And—I'm so sorry about everything.'

Emerald nodded dully, and went with Claire to fetch the children, and to take her leave of Saul. Both Timothy and Selina were in tears as they drove away in the pony and trap, and Emerald left them to weep for a while before she asked, 'Are you good at keeping secrets?'

'Y-yes,' Timothy sniffed. 'Se-Selina is good at keeping secrets too.'

'In that case,' Emerald said with studied casualness, 'the three of us will set out for the store again at some later date, and it will not be our fault if we should happen to take the wrong fork and end up visiting your aunt and uncle again.'

The children were stunned into silence for a moment. Then Timothy said, 'I shan't tell Uncle Judah that we lost our way. Selina won't tell him either.'

'Good.' Emerald shrugged aside any feelings of guilt at conspiring with the children to defy and deceive Judah. The children had been deprived of enough in their short lives; they should not also be deprived of all contact with the two people who had taken the place of their parents in their hearts.

Besides, Emerald wanted to see Andrew. She wanted to hear from his own lips that he still loved her, even though it was too late. That much comfort, at least, was owed to her.

She had forgiven him everything. It would have taken a saint to withstand not only the pressure which Saul, his employer and benefactor, was putting on him, but also Claire's haunting beauty. And Andrew was no saint; he had been vulnerable and lonely and dogged by a sense of failure at the time.

After that day, the children were always willing to do Emerald's bidding, but they showed no signs of transferring their love to her, and she did not expect them to. Now that she had conceded defeat in the battle for their emotional dependence on her, Emerald was content to share with Alice the daily task of looking after their physical welfare.

No opportunity arose to take them again on a secret visit to Claire and Saul, so Emerald occupied her spare time by practising her riding.

She was discovering that she had a natural aptitude as a horse-woman, and had long ago exchanged her first, sluggish old mare for a spirited young gelding. She was riding further and further afield each day.

A restless irritation claimed her, and she could no longer deny that it was somehow caused by Judah's continued absence from Coorabee Creek. She found that, whenever she was seated upon the veranda, her glance would stray to the furthest point of the track, watching for signs of his return. One morning, in revolt against such useless and abortive waiting and watching, she decided to ask Hettie for a packed lunch and to ride as far as she could, spending the entire day away from home.

Towards noon she was beginning to regret her impulsive plan. The sun was hot and searing as she rode along a track which was no more than a bed of thick dust which stung her eyes, and then picked her away through dense bush and over steep hills. The air was stagnant and sultry, and myriads of insects filled the air with their never-ending hum.

She was following what was obviously an old cattle track, but there was evidence everywhere of the sheep which Judah had brought on to the land. They grazed in isolated flocks, and every now and again she spied, in the distance, the huts which were obviously used by convicts who acted as shepherds.

Tired and hungry, she made her way to one such cluster of huts with the intention of sitting in their shade to eat her picnic lunch. The rude dwellings seemed deserted; the convicts obviously used them only at night.

She rounded a rocky ridge towards the huts and dismounted, hobbling her horse. Then she carried her picnic hamper towards the shade cast by the huts.

Just as she was about to make herself comfortable against one of the mud walls, she heard a moaning sound coming from inside one hut, and she went to investigate.

It was a low, bark-roofed building of the crudest construction. It was so dark inside that she was temporarily blinded, and she felt rather than saw that the floor was of bare earth. The moaning sound was coming from the furthest corner of the hut. It was only when her eyes had become accustomed to the gloom that she was able to make out the wretched creature chained and tethered to an iron stake driven into the ground inside the hut.

It was an old man with grizzled grey hair, dressed in rags. His face was lined and seamed with a combination of sun and wind and physical hardship. He had stifled his moans, and was watching Emerald with resigned, hopeless eyes.

'You poor creature,' she said gently. 'Who are you, and why are you being kept here?'

'Nat Williams, ma'am.' He stared yearningly at the picnic hamper which Emerald was still carrying. 'Ma'am—a drink of water—please?'

'I've only buttermilk.' She unpacked the hamper swiftly, and held the flask to his lips.

'Thank you, ma'am,' he said when he had all but drained the flask. 'I apologise for my greed—but I've had neither wet nor dry pass my lips these twenty-four hours past . . .'

'Good lord!' Emerald reached inside the hamper for bread and cheese and slices of beef, and watched him eating voraciously.

He looked slightly less wretched after he had been fed. Emerald warned herself against too-easy feelings of outrage at his fate. He might seem too old and spent to have committed some desperate deed, and he was obviously educated, but there was no doubt that he was being confined in irons inside the hut as a punishment, so he must have done something to merit it. But not, she added to herself, being starved into the bargain . . .

'I know you must be one of the convicts, Nat,' she said. 'I would have thought an old man like you would have had better sense than to give the farm constable reason for punishing you like this?'

'An old man, ma'am? I'm in my forty-second year! And yes, I should have had the sense not to cross the farm constable, me being a ticket-of-leave man, and knowing that the farm constable could lose me my ticket.'

He spoke with a searing, sardonic bitterness. He was obviously intelligent and articulate.

'Why were you transported in the first place, Nat?'

'I was a clerk in a shipping office, ma'am, and some money went missing.'

'I see.' Emerald did not ask whether he had been guilty or not, but she reflected with compassion on the harshness of penal servitude which could make a man of forty-two appear to be twenty years older. Then she probed once more, 'What did you do to merit this punishment, Nat?'

'Ma'am, we were all starving. We'd received short rations again last Saturday and by Wednesday they had all been eaten. We were forced to dig for wild roots, the way we'd seen the Blacks do, in order to remain alive. And starving as we were, ma'am, we were still expected to do our usual work. So I took it upon myself to lead a deputation to the farm constable, to ask for the full rations we are entitled to. He flogged me first, and then he chained me up in here without food or water.'

'But—but this is terrible! I'd no idea . . .'

'I dare say you hadn't, ma'am. I suppose I was lucky—the farm constable could have seen to it that I got six months in Government instead.'

'Six months in Government?' Emerald echoed.

'An extra six months added to my sentence, spent labouring in irons in a road gang, and with the loss of my ticket.'

Emerald stared at him in appalled silence for a while. 'I understood the farm constables are, themselves, ex-convicts,' she said at last. 'I would have thought that would have made them more sympathetic to those still serving their sentences.'

'Not a bit of it, ma'am. It's the worse kind of ex-convict who applies to become a farm constable. He knows he's going to be hated and despised, but he cares nothing for that. There's money in being a farm constable, ma'am. Money to be made from graft, from selling the convicts' rations, from informing or bounty-hunting of bushrangers.'

'Where,' Emerald asked grimly, 'is this particular farm constable to be found at the moment?'

'He and the convicts in his charge are half an hour's ride away from here to the north, putting up barricades to stop the sheep from falling into a ravine.'

'I'll go and have a word with him.'

'Ma'am,' Nat Williams interrupted urgently. 'If you were to tell him what you've learnt from me, it would go all the worse for me.'

'I shan't mention you, Nat. I merely want to be able to find out his name from his own lips, so that I may inform my husband about his activities. I am married to Mr Judah Renshaw, and as soon as he returns to Coorabee Creek I shall see to it that this particular farm constable is removed from his post!'

'God bless you, Mrs Renshaw. And—if ever Nat Williams can be of service to you . . .'

'I'll remember, Nat. Goodbye, and thank you.'

A few minutes later she was spurring the gelding grimly on in the direction which Nat Williams had indicated. She rode along the well-worn cattle track which skirted the mountainside and then suddenly became a gulley over which large trees cast a green gloom. And then, unexpectedly, she came upon the barricades which the convicts had been putting up, and she could glimpse the ravine which yawned just beyond them.

She followed the line of the barricades, but she heard the convicts long before she saw them. They manifested themselves, not by the sound of saw and pick and shovel, but by a low, moaning murmur of helpless anger and frustration. And above this sound, Emerald heard the whine of a whip lashing through the air, followed by the unmistakable thud as it made contact with human flesh.

She urged the gelding on, gripped by blind fury. No one noticed her approaching. The convicts stood together in a bunch, their blood-shot eyes filled with numb hatred as they watched a brutish man with a coarse-featured face bring the whip down again and again upon the bare back of what seemed to be no more than a youth.

Emerald scrambled from the horse and ran towards the farm constable, too enraged to fear that that same cruel whip might land on her own flesh.

'How dare you!' she shouted, and the farm constable spun around, open-mouthed with astonishment. Something must have warned him who she was, for he began with whining self-justification,

'Found the wretch tryin' to run away, ma'am.'

She glanced at the youth's blood-stained back, and then, like an avenging fury, she launched herself at the farm constable, wresting the whip from his suddenly slack fingers. Before he had guessed her intentions she was wielding it against him, and each lash she inflicted on his cringing body was raggedly cheered by the convicts.

At last her rage had spent itself. She threw the whip down with a gesture of contempt, and faced the farm constable. 'What is your name?'

Hatred blazed in his eyes. 'Jem Connors.'

'Well, Jem Connors, your days here are numbered! And in case you should be thinking of soothing your own ruffled feelings by making these poor wretches suffer even more, be warned— I intend to have my husband question them personally, and give them the chance to lay information against you!'

The cheers of the convicts ringing in her ears, she mounted and galloped away, back to the house, to look for Murphy.

But he was away, checking on other convict outposts, and not expected back until the late hours. Acting on her own authority, Emerald ordered one of the homestead convicts to load the wagonette with food supplies and to take it to the convict camp from which she had just returned.

The experience had left a nasty taste in her mouth, and that night she found herself unable to sleep. She lit a candle, and lay staring at the cubicle with its sofa which should have been occupied by Judah. Why didn't he come home? Did he really believe it was reasonable behaviour, staying away for so long from his bride of only a few days . . .

She caught herself up on the thought, astonished at herself. Why *should* he be in a hurry to return to a marriage which was not a marriage at all? To an uncomfortable bed on a sofa, which he had to sneak into after she was asleep and sneak out of again before she awakened? She sighed. He was probably regretting their ill-fated marriage as bitterly as she was.

Her thoughts turned to Andrew. Why had he not come to see her, to assure her of his love? He must be aware that Judah was away. But perhaps Judah had forbidden him to set foot on his land . . .

The next morning her longing to see Andrew decided her to take the children for another visit to Claire and Saul Renshaw. But before she could begin the elaborate pretence of needing to set out for the township, Judah returned home.

Emerald looked at him, his teeth very white in his tanned, dust-stained face as he swept each of the children in turn exuberantly into the air, and felt herself filled by an inexplicable anger.

When he released the children and turned to her, she said tartly, 'So you've deigned to come home! I suppose you were sated with pleasure . . .'

'*Pleasure!*' He thrust a hand through his silver-gilt hair. 'I went to Port Phillip to buy a very expensive prize Merino ram, and I've been acting as nursemaid to it ever since!' His eyes shone. 'Would you like to see it?'

'I've no interest in sheep, thank you!' She was still consumed by an anger whose cause she did not understand, and told herself that it was because his homecoming had thwarted her plan to see Andrew.

'I fail to see how the purchase of a single sheep could have taken up so much time,' she went on. 'And while you've been away, your convicts have been starved and flogged and tied up like animals!'

He listened grimly while she recounted her discovery, and his expression altered only once, when she described how she had turned the farm constable's whip upon himself. Then his lips twitched slightly, but when she had finished, he merely said,

'This isn't rural England, my dear Emerald. Keeping convicts disciplined isn't easy, and the men in charge of them have to be strong and hard and sometimes, of necessity, brutal.'

'So you intend doing nothing about it?' she cried, outraged.

'I didn't say that. I'll look into it. In the meantime, I forbid you to ride out such a long distance again by yourself, do you hear?'

'You're very good at forbidding, aren't you, Judah,' she observed acidly. 'But, for twenty sovereigns, there's a limit to the obedience you can expect from me!'

He muttered something under his breath which sounded like an oath, and strode away.

In the days which followed, Emerald saw very little of him. He was always at work somewhere on the station with Murphy, and did not arrive home until just before dinner. Their nights assumed a new pattern. Now, pleading exhaustion, Judah would retire almost immediately after dinner, and Emerald would sit in the living-room, sewing by the light of a lantern until she judged that he was asleep in the dressing cubicle, before she crept quietly into the bedroom and undressed in the dark. He was always gone by the time she woke in the morning.

One night, after she had sat up late over her sewing as usual, Emerald found it impossible to sleep. The day had been excessively hot and sultry, and darkness had done nothing to lessen the oppressive atmosphere.

Desperate for a breath of air, and careful not to disturb Judah who was asleep in the dressing cubicle, she rose and tiptoed from the room.

It was only marginally cooler on the veranda than it had been inside the house, and a distant rumble of thunder warned her that the intense heat of the day had presaged a threatened storm. She leant against the railing, staring out into the night.

'What do you want?' Judah's voice growled at her from behind.

She whirled round. A sudden flash of lightning showed him stretched out on the bench of latticed rawhide, his folded arms behind his head forming a cushion.

'Jude . . . Judah . . .' she stammered. 'What are you doing here? I thought . . . I was sure you were in bed . . .'

'We don't know much about one another's sleeping habits, do we,' he observed morosely.

'Have you—decided to sleep out here from now on?'

'I don't know *what* I've decided.' He rose, and came to stand beside her. 'Have you any conception,' he demanded with sudden roughness, 'of the torment you put me through nightly?'

'I—have never done anything . . .' she began defensively.

'No, that's right, you haven't.' He gave a brief, savage laugh. 'I've tried going to bed late, and I've tried going to bed early, but it all comes to the same in the end. I don't know which is worse—to creep in when you are asleep, and watch your unaware face by candle-light, and see your hair fanned out upon the pillow. You didn't know I did that, did you?'

She said nothing, glad that he could not read the truth in her eyes.

'So then I tried going to bed first,' his voice continued in the darkness. 'But it meant that I was awake by five, when it was already growing light. And you would be perfectly visible from that cursed sofa of mine. During the heat of the night you would have flung the covers off, and you would lie there, in the most abandoned pose ever to try the self-control of a man!'

He moved suddenly, drawing her roughly against him. 'God Almighty, it's more than flesh and blood can stand!'

'Judah, please . . .'

Ignoring her protest, he picked her up in his arms and moved to the bench. His mouth claimed hers hungrily, lighting a fire in her blood, and she was capable of only a token resistance as his hand slid beneath her night-gown, cupping her breasts and sliding down to fondle the flatness of her stomach.

A clap of thunder almost deafened them, bringing her to her senses, and she wrenched herself away from him. She had almost surrendered to him in what was no more than lust, betraying her love for Andrew, betraying her own self-respect.

The landscape around them was suddenly lit up by the most unearthly light playing across the skies. Then, with no further warning, the rain came—falling in a solid, blinding sheet. Within seconds the area surrounding the house resembled a foaming brown lake as the lightning played upon it.

'Is . . . is this usual?' she asked Judah, thankful to the elements for having saved her from utter self-degradation.

'No. I've never known anything like it . . .'

He stopped, and struck his forehead with a clenched fist. *'Oh my God!'*

'What is it?'

'Saul's house—the tributary of the Murrumbidgee . . .'

She understood instantly. The river had never been known to dry up, Claire had said. And in this terrible, unprecedented cloudburst it would become a bank of foam sweeping away everything in its path.

'*Andrew* . . .' she began, her voice shrill with panic.

Judah gave her a searing look. 'I'll save his miserable skin too, never fear. You'd better pray that I'm not too late.'

Then he swung himself down the veranda steps and began to race through the blinding rain towards the stables.

CHAPTER SIX

No one slept during the remainder of that terrible night.

Emerald stayed on the veranda and watched Judah on his horse battling his way through the rain towards Saul's station, followed by several of his men. Sporadic flashes of lightning vividly and dramatically silhouetted the horsemen against the storm-dark sky.

Convicts ran through the battering rain, calming the horses which were going berserk with fear in the stables, struggling to get as many as possible of the sheep in the immediate vicinity under shelter of some kind.

Alice found Emerald there on the veranda, numb with fear, and touched her arm. 'Madam, you'd better come. The children are hysterical.'

Emerald didn't move immediately. Instead, she said through chattering teeth, 'Jude . . . Judah has ridden to his brother's house. But surely . . . surely they would have evacuated the house in plenty of time . . . ?'

'Not necessarily, madam,' Alice explained in a sober voice. 'I think we are getting the brunt of the storm. Mr Saul's station is probably on the edge of it. They will have had no warning of the volume of river water which is rushing down towards them.'

Emerald closed her eyes. So it was, literally, a race against time . . .

She forced herself to enter the house, and mechanically set about calming the children's fears. A fierce wind had sprung up now, and was plucking ominously at the roof. Emerald held the children close and tried to blot out the hellish sounds of the elements, tried not to think of Judah and his men arriving at Saul's station to find the house battered out of existence and the drowned bodies of its occupants floating in the flood-waters.

In the kitchen, Hettie and her helpers were keeping tea on the brew for the stockmen who came in from time to time, soaked to the skin and bone-weary, gasping for refreshment. News percolated through to Emerald that every small gully and creek in the vicinity had been turned into a foaming miniature river, and that several sheep had been drowned.

Although the storm was still at its height, sheer fatigue caused the children to fall asleep after a while, and Emerald and Alice carried them to their beds.

'Madam,' Alice said afterwards, 'You look worn out. Why don't you, too, try to get some sleep?'

'I couldn't. Not until I know that—everyone—is safe.' She looked at the housekeeper, who could so easily have been her friend if their circumstances had been different. 'Alice, would you keep me company in the living-room? I dread being alone with my fears . . .'

'Certainly, madam,' Alice said with quiet understanding. 'With your permission, I shall ask one of the maids to bring us some tea.'

They sat together, mistress and convict servant,

drinking tea and listening to the fury of the storm. The need to blot out her own terrified thoughts caused Emerald to broach a subject which she had always been too reticent to allude to in the past.

'Alice—I know that you were transported for the manslaughter of your husband, and that he was a brutal man. I also know that it is an unwritten rule never to question a . . . a convict, but I would deem it a privilege if you were to tell me something of your circumstances. I am not merely prying, you understand . . .'

'I understand perfectly, madam.' Alice smiled faintly, and her eyes held compassion. 'You fear for Mr Renshaw's safety, and you need something to take your mind off the matter. I have no objection to telling you about myself. My father was a curate, and I was the only child of the marriage.'

'A curate!' Emerald echoed. 'My father was also a clergyman! I have always felt that we had things in common . . . But you told me once that your father was a brutal man.'

'He would not have admitted to the charge of brutality,' Alice said with an edge of cynicism to her voice. 'He would have called it just chastisement, and talked about not spoiling a child by sparing the rod. The truth was that I was a bitter disappointment to him. He had wanted a son, you see, madam, and after my birth my mother was told that she dared not risk having more children. So my father had a double reason for hating me. I was not the son he had wanted, and my birth was also the reason why he was forced to live a life of celibacy afterwards. At the time I knew nothing of these matters, of course, but now I realise that he was a passionate man, and his frustration must have been intense. He relieved it by beating me for the slightest transgression.'

'Poor Alice,' Emerald said softly.

The other woman shrugged. 'I did not pity myself. I assumed that all children were treated in the same manner. My father tutored me himself, so that I had almost no contact with others of my age, and nothing else by which to judge matters.'

'But did you not hate your father for what he did to you?'

'Indeed no. My mother understood what motivated him, and while I'm sure she tried to spare me as much as she could, she did not wish me to hate him. So she instilled into me that I should respect him, and that everything he did was for my own good. I suppose fear and respect became mixed up in my mind, so that I could not tell one from the other.'

Alice sighed. 'But the result was that when I was eighteen and I began to receive proposals of marriage from suitors, I instinctively chose as a husband the one man who was most like my father. I did not recognise his cruelty for what it was. I confused it with strength and authority.'

'Yes, I think I understand.' Emerald was silent for a moment. 'You had no children, I take it?'

Alice's voice was toneless when she replied. 'I was expecting our first child when my husband returned home, once again the worse for drink. He worked as a clerk to an attorney-at-law, and in the evenings he would frequent a low ale-house or a gin-palace before coming home. I began, more and more, to dread his nightly return . . . No one among our friends or his colleagues suspected that he drank, or that he beat me regularly, and I did my best to keep the truth from them. I suppose it was a form of pride . . .' Her voice tailed off, and she retreated into silence, the corners of her mouth turned down.

'You said you were expecting a baby,' Emerald prompted gently. 'Was *that* when . . . ?'

'Yes, madam, that was when I killed him.' There was no emotion in Alice's voice. 'I was trying to protect my baby. He had grabbed me by the hair with one hand, and was punching me in the stomach with the other. We were in the kitchen at the time. I saw the knife lying on the table, and I reached for it . . .' Her control broke then, and she sank her head in her hands.

Emerald rose and went to her, placing her arms about the convict girl. After a while Alice composed herself, and went on, 'I killed him, but not in time to save my baby. I lost it the day afterwards, in gaol.'

'I am so very sorry, Alice,' Emerald whispered.

Alice gave her a watery smile. 'Perhaps it was for the best. The baby was a girl, and if she had lived she would have had to share my time in gaol, and who knows what her fate would have been after I had been transported? I shall still be young enough to have children when I have worked my ticket. I comfort myself with that thought.'

'And you are so beautiful,' Emerald said spontaneously, 'that you won't lack suitors!'

Alice acknowledged the comment with a smile, and changed the subject. 'I think the storm is blowing itself out, madam.'

Emerald moved to the window. Dawn was lightening the sky, and the storm did indeed seem to be abating, with the sound of thunder growing more distant.

Soon the sun rose winsomely over the horizon, shining from a clear sky and belying the ferocious drama which had played itself out during the night. Only the brown muddy water which still swirled around everywhere, and the bloated bodies of drowned sheep which marred the immediate landscape, bore evidence of the storm.

Emerald heard Alice's voice behind her. 'I think, madam, with your permission I had better go and lend a hand in the kitchen now.'

'Very well, Alice. And—thank you for keeping me company, and for honouring me with your confidence.'

'Thank *you*, madam, for your sympathy and understanding. And please try not to worry too much. I am sure that Mr Renshaw will be safe—that he will have reached Mr Saul and his wife before the flood-water struck their house.'

But would *Andrew* be safe? Emerald asked herself. Would Judah have gone out of his way to rescue him, as well as Saul and Claire?

Emerald's nerves were at screaming-point as she watched the horizon. And then she saw it—a dray drawn by bullocks slowly making its way towards the house.

The children had woken up again and were weeping with fatigue and with the memory of fear. Leaving Alice to comfort them, Emerald ran through the mud and the water to the stables, and saddled her gelding, and then rode to meet the dray.

She expelled her breath in a fervent sigh when she saw that Andrew was driving the dray. He gave her a brief, weary salute; she had time only to acknowledge it with a look of tenderness and heartfelt gratitude for his safety when Judah swung his legs from the back of the canvas-canopied dray, and demanded, 'Is my ram safe?'

'Your ram?' she echoed stupidly.

'My prize ram, the one I paid a fortune for in Port Phillip.' He looked tired and strained and on edge. 'Of course, I forgot,' he added with a brief laugh. 'You are not interested in sheep. Let me have your horse; you can ride on the dray with Saul and Claire.'

She dismounted, and he swung himself into the saddle and streaked towards the house to reassure himself of the safety of his prize ram. Emerald gathered her skirts and climbed on the back of the dray.

Saul was lying on a board covered by a palliasse, and Claire sat beside him. Both of them looked gaunt and hollow-eyed, and were obviously still suffering from shock.

'Judah arrived just in time,' Saul said. 'We were asleep, unaware of the danger . . .'

Claire shuddered. 'By the time Saul had been carried to the dray, and a few of our possessions hurled on to it, the water began to rise. It was like a living, monstrous thing as it burst its banks . . . Andrew spurred the bullocks on, but we felt as though we were trapped in space and time. I looked out from the back of the dray, and I could see our house being torn apart as though it had been constructed of matchwood . . .' Her voice caught.

'We'll have a better house built,' Saul comforted her. 'On higher ground, further away from the river.'

She turned her wedding ring round and round on her finger. 'But in the meantime . . . in the meantime, we'll have to stay in Judah's house.'

'And a good thing,' her husband said briskly. 'The scandal-mongers will be silenced when it is known that we are living with my brother, and that Andrew is a frequent visitor there.'

'A frequent visitor?' Emerald echoed. 'Will Judah countenance that?'

'He will have to. Andrew is my manager, accountable to me, and he receives his instructions from me. Since I am physically unable to go to him, he will have to come to me.'

'If the house has been destroyed,' Emerald asked, 'where will Andrew live?'

'He and the servants will have to construct temporary shelters. He is to return just as soon as he has delivered Claire and myself to Judah's house.'

So there was to be no longed-for private talk with Andrew, as Emerald had been hoping. Indeed, he was far too busy re-loading the dray with emergency rations for himself and the servants left behind on Saul's station to exchange so much as a word with her, and she stifled her disappointment as she went into the house to give orders for a room to be prepared for Saul and Claire, and for breakfast to be served to them there.

The two children were overjoyed at this unexpected reunion with their uncle and aunt, and could not be dragged away from their side. Emerald left them together and went into the dining-room, where she found a gaunt-faced Judah enjoying a solitary breakfast.

'Is your ram safe?' she asked.

He nodded. 'Thanks to Murphy. But God knows

how many of the sheep in the outlying runs have been drowned. There are bound to have been losses, and the ram will be doubly valuable now. I plan to use him to cross-breed with my surviving ewes and start a new strain with a high yield of wool.' He gave her a cyncial, tired grin. 'Sorry. You're not interested.'

'I confess I'm far more interested in people than in sheep,' she answered pointedly. 'I have been wondering how the wretched convicts in the outlying pastures have been faring during the storm. I told you about the way they were being beaten and starved, but you dismissed it.'

'I did not dismiss it. I questioned the convicts, and they had no complaints about the farm constables or about their rations.'

'Can't you see, they were too afraid of reprisals to tell you the truth? What about the poor young lad whom I caught Jem Connors flogging?'

Judah rose. 'That poor young lad had tried to escape. If he had not been publicly punished, it would have encouraged other convicts to try escaping. And do you know what happens to escaped convicts? They become bushrangers, with every man's hand against them, and liable to be shot on sight! Don't you think a salutary flogging is preferable to that fate?'

'I think this is a cruel, barbaric country, and that you are equally cruel and barbaric!'

'You gave every sign of enjoying the barbaric side of my nature last night,' he reminded her with deliberate malice. 'Until you remembered your beloved Standish!'

She flushed, and retaliated with equally deliberate brutality. 'You paid twenty sovereigns for me.

Last night I allowed you a small return on your money. That was all. I do not like to feel indebted to anyone.'

His face had hardened. 'I see. Since you view our relationship entirely in terms of money, it will no doubt have struck you that Fate has rendered my investment in you totally profitless. Claire will be remaining here for an indefinite period, and there is nothing I can do to stop her from influencing and caring for the children again. You, my dear Emerald, have turned out to be a pig in a poke!'

Her face flaming, she turned angrily away from him and went in search of the children. As she had expected, their disturbed night, the drama of the storm and then the excitement of their reunion with their uncle and aunt had been too much for them and they were almost asleep on their feet.

After Emerald had seen them into bed, she returned to Claire and Saul's room to make certain that they had everything they required. The door stood half open, showing that Claire was not in the room, and that Judah was seated by his brother's side.

'I'm going to have a chair designed and built for you!' she heard Judah say with gruff affection. 'A chair with wheels. You must be sick of lying in a damned bed!'

'And where would I go in this wheeled chair you have in mind?' Saul asked gently, with no trace of self-pity. 'Of what greater use would I be?'

Judah swore under his breath. Then, rising, he gripped his brother by the shoulder. 'At least it would be less boring for you. I'll give my attention to it as soon as I get back.' He turned his head, and saw Emerald.

'I shall be away from home for several nights,' he told her. 'I have to ride out with Murphy and some of the men to check on the outlying sheep runs.'

'I see,' she returned without expression, her fingers crossed behind her back. Perhaps Andrew would come to see Saul while Judah was away, so that at long last she could be alone with him and tell him what was in her heart and her mind.

An idea had occurred to her, filling her with excitement whenever she thought of it. Judah had referred to her as a pig in a poke; he was as disillusioned about their marriage as she herself was. He would not object to being rid of her for good. And even in this colony it should be possible to have their marriage annulled, so that she and Andrew could marry.

But since there was no sign of Andrew, she was forced to keep her plans to herself. Once or twice she thought about confiding in Claire, but some instinct always stopped her. Instead, on an impulse one day she saddled her horse and began to ride out in the direction of Saul's station. Since Andrew failed to call, she would go and see him instead, and put her proposition to him.

But Emerald had just turned into the fork which would take her to Saul's station when, to her utmost dismay, she saw the wagonette coming towards her, with Murphy driving and Judah sitting beside him. Judah had obviously taken time off from checking on his sheep runs to see how things were going on Saul's station.

There was no way of evading him, no way of hiding the truth about her intended destination. For a moment she considered summary flight, but pride forced her to rein in and wait, to brazen the matter out.

As the wagonette reached her and she saw Judah's face, she wished that she *had* taken flight instead. At his curt command, Murphy reined in the horses, and Judah said, 'How very thoughtful of you to ride out and meet me like this!'

His words had probably been chosen for Murphy's benefit, and were intended to be taken at face value. But because Judah was not a man who could put on a false front when his passion was aroused, the statement sounded corrosive and menacing, instead of the pleasantry he had meant it to be taken for.

'Murphy will ride your gelding home,' he continued, 'while you join me.'

The overseer had already relinquished the reins and was alighting from the wagonette, and there was nothing Emerald could do but dismount, and take up the passenger seat beside Judah.

She waited nervously for him to say something, but he remained ominously silent even after Murphy had galloped away. It came to her suddenly that Judah was in the grip of such a murderous rage that he did not trust himself to say or do anything for the moment.

When he did make a move, it was to pick up the reins and whip up the horses unsparingly. He was, she knew, venting his fury at her on the poor beasts, and she could not allow it to go on.

'Judah, slow down for pity's sake!' she cried. 'Do you want the horses to drop dead in their shafts?'

Some kind of sanity returned to him, for he slackened the reins and allowed the tired horses to trot the rest of the way home.

'You were on your way to see Andrew Standish, were you not?' The words were ground out between his teeth.

It would have been futile to deny it. 'Yes, I was.' Defiantly, she added, 'I merely wished to speak to him.'

'Indeed? About what? The inclement weather we have recently been experiencing, perhaps?' His voice was harsh and sarcastic.

'No. I—I have never tried to hide from you the way I feel about Andrew . . .'

'That is true.' He grabbed her arm in a bruising hold. 'I don't expect much for my twenty sovereigns, Emerald, but I *do* expect—and demand—that you should keep up appearances! And that does not include paying sneaking visits to Andrew Standish!'

They had reached the house, but he made no attempt to help her as she alighted from the wagonette. He leant down towards her, and added in a voice which reminded her of splintered ice, 'Just remember—you are my property, and I do not share with Andrew Standish anything that belongs to me—*no matter how little I might value it!*'

'Oh God, how I *hate* you, Judah!' she cried with passion.

'Hate away!' He bared his teeth in a malevolent grimace. 'Just leave Andrew Standish to conduct his adulterous association exclusively with Claire!'

'You're wrong about Andrew and Claire! And you're not fit to mention his name . . .'

She stopped as Judah raised the whip, and for one terrified, incredulous moment she thought he meant to use it upon her. Instead, he cracked it viciously in the air, and the horses sped with the wagonette towards the stables.

Emerald tried to put that ugly scene behind her, and continued to wait for Andrew. Judah returned to his work on the outlying runs, and remained away from home, but somehow she could not scrape up sufficient courage to try and repeat an attempted visit to Andrew. Instead, she watched the horizon daily, and in the meantime tried to console herself with the company of Saul and Claire.

On the surface, she and Claire became friends, but there was something about Judah's sister-in-law, something enigmatic upon which Emerald could not put a finger, which prevented any true intimacy between them. Eventually Emerald ascribed it to the difference in their social backgrounds.

Claire came of an aristocratic family, but her father was only a second son, and he'd had four children to provide for, so that she had had no dowry to speak of. When Saul visited England, and mutual friends introduced them, he hadn't cared about her lack of a dowry.

'I saw only her beauty and her goodness and the warm nature which she hid behind that dignified air of hers,' was the way Saul put it to Emerald one afternoon.

His wife flushed faintly. 'You saw what you wanted to see, my dearest.'

'Don't you ever miss your family?' Emerald asked curiously, having no family of her own to miss.

Claire appeared not to have heard the question, and gave her attention instead to the children who had just entered the room. 'Ah, my darlings! Would you like Auntie Claire to tell you a story? Come and sit on my lap!'

Emerald could not help becoming more and more aware of the fact that Claire spoiled the children dreadfully. It was no wonder they were so attached to her, for she pandered to their every whim. Indeed, there was something constricting and smothering about her love for them, as though she were using them to make up for everything she herself was missing in life.

In an effort to restore some kind of balance, Emerald began to set them daily lessons so that they would at least receive discipline in some form.

To begin with they were unco-operative and resentful. Characteristically, Claire sided with them. 'They're no more than babies, Emerald! Surely all this learning can wait until they are older?'

'This is precisely the age when they are most receptive to learning,' Emerald said firmly, and continued with her efforts.

Gradually, because they were intelligent and quick to learn, and because she turned their lessons into games, she captured the children's interest. She encouraged them to bring her wild flowers and small insects, and used these to instruct them in biology. An odd relationship began to blossom between them. Claire was still the one who petted and indulged them, but Emerald had become a friend whose company they voluntarily sought.

One day when the three of them were outside on one of their rambles, looking for interesting specimens to study, they came unexpectedly upon a dead sheep lying in a gully. It could not have been a victim of the storm, for it had only recently died. Ignorant though she was, Emerald sensed that Judah ought to know about this, so she sent the children home and went to look for some of the convicts in charge of matters on the home station.

'Do you know where your master is at the moment?' she asked.

'No, ma'am, he could be anywheres on one of the outlying runs.'

She bit her lip. 'Is there any way in which you could locate him quickly?'

'Not really, ma'am. In so many thousands of acres, 'twould be like lookin' for a needle in a haystack.'

They were clearly unwilling to make the effort to search for Judah, and did not consider the death of the sheep to be significant. Emerald decided that she had over-reacted. Even sheep must die sometimes of natural causes.

When the convicts did make a concerted attempt to locate Judah the following morning, it was not because of the sheep which had died. Two dragoon officers had appeared at the station at dawn, resplendent in scarlet uniforms, and announced that they had travelled from Sydney with a message from the Governor. Judah had been gazetted as a magistrate of the territory, and it was necessary for him to be sworn in at the township courthouse.

After a morning spent in fanning out over the property, the convicts succeeded in finding Judah, and he returned home, dusty and tired and not in the best of humours.

There was no opportunity for Emerald to tell him about the dead sheep, even if she had thought of it, for the dragoon officers claimed his attention.

'It's a great honour,' Judah commented, looking anything but gratified, and Emerald guessed that he felt irked by the inroads on his time which his new duties would be making.

Just before he left with the dragoons for the courthouse, Judah kissed Emerald on the cheek for the sake of appearances, and then swept each of the children up in his arms, holding them shoulder-high.

'Be good,' he warned with mock severity. 'For when I return, I shall be a magistrate, and it will be my duty to punish wrong-doers by clapping them in gaol!'

They giggled, and watched the three men riding away, but they were far more impressed by the dragoons than by their uncle's new exalted position. Timothy announced that he meant to be a dragoon when he grew up, and Selina wept because her sex debarred her for ever from that glamorous profession, and was consoled only when Emerald pointed out that she could do the next best thing and marry a dragoon.

'Let us carry on with our lessons,' she added, settling herself down on the veranda. The lesson this afternoon was in arithmetic, and she was using small pebbles as counters to make the sums she was setting them less abstract.

Suddenly the sound of approaching hoof-beats broke through their absorption, and Emerald looked up, surprised that Judah should be returning so soon. Instead, with a wildly beating heart, she saw that it was Andrew.

Speaking through suddenly dry lips, she said, 'Timothy, you and Selina may go and play. We've done enough lessons for the moment.'

'I can't, Aunt Emerald! Selina still owes me two pebbles.'

'She can pay you back tomorrow. Alice told me that one of the barn cats has had kittens; go and see if the mother will let you have a peep at them.'

At the prospect of this treat the children left eagerly, and Emerald found herself facing Andrew.

There was constraint in the smile which he gave her. 'I've called to see Saul . . .'

'Claire is reading aloud to him in their room. Andrew—I've longed so much to see you, to speak to you . . . There is so much we have to discuss, but first of all I must tell you that my marriage is a hollow mockery, not a marriage at all.'

Pain clouded his eyes. 'Don't make me feel more guilty than I already do, Emerald . . .'

'Oh, but I don't blame you for anything! Saul and Claire have both explained things to me, and I can see how it all came about. I even understand the reason for your lies to me. You had, at all cost, to prevent me from walking into the middle of the scandal which had flared up. If anyone is guilty, it is I. I gave you no chance to explain; I leapt to conclusions and hurried into a disastrous marriage with Judah. But all is not lost, darling Andrew. I can see a way out for us. Judah is as disenchanted with our so-called marriage as I am, and I'm sure he'll agree to an annulment. Then you and I . . .'

'No, Emerald.' His voice was so low that it was barely audible. He covered his face briefly with his hand.

'Do you doubt that Judah will consent to an annulment? I assure you, he does not love me any more than I love him!'

Andrew removed his hand from his face and she saw that his eyes held a tormented expression. 'I have done you too much harm already to allow you to continue under a delusion, Emerald. I couldn't let you complicate your life even further. I'm in love with Claire.'

Emerald felt for the veranda rail behind her, and clung to it, staring at him. She moistened her dry lips. '*No*! Claire and Saul have explained everything to me.'

'Claire lied to you,' he interrupted quietly, and sighed. 'For Saul's sake, both of us have been lying for a long time.'

'I . . . don't understand,' she whispered.

'We did try to end our affair after the scandal broke. But something beyond our control had been kindled into life, and much as we tried to kill it . . .' Andrew shook his head. 'To begin with, Saul had thrown us together, and when the scandal engulfed us he wanted to declare publicly that our affair had his blessing and consent. Claire and I knew that we had to stop him, for if he did as he threatened the three of us would have been ostracised for the rest of our lives. It would not have stopped at a mere scandal. No one would have traded with us and Saul would have been financially ruined. So we did the only thing we could think of. We told him that our affair had meant nothing.'

Andrew made a helpless gesture. 'Afterwards, neither of us could forget the way he had looked when we told him that. He had looked like a proud, whole man again instead of a cripple. So how could we openly resume the affair? How could we take away what we had given him?'

His words fell upon Emerald's spirit like stones.

'You . . .' she began, her voice sounding unreal to her own ears. 'The—affair is still continuing, in secret . . .'

'It's not something either of us is proud of,' Andrew said heavily. 'And we both know how hopeless it is. But we are trapped by the feeling between us.'

Emerald's entire body had begun to shake. 'You talk of being trapped, of being hopeless . . . *What about me, Andrew?* I crossed half the world to be with you!'

Tears were coursing down her cheeks now and he moved towards her, drawing her into his arms. 'Oh God, Emerald, if you knew how I've hated hurting you . . . I'm sorry. So sorry.'

She stood there within the circle of his arms, too devastated, desolate and utterly bereft to move or to do anything but allow pain to wash over her.

He kissed her gently, and even though her mind knew that he was only offering her comfort, her treacherous heart was transported back to the past, away from the heat and the dust and the flies, from the raw ugliness of so much in the colony, away from the bitter reality of rejection. The two of them were back once more in the Standishes' elegant London home, stealing sweet forbidden kisses on the darkened landing while the ball was in progress. She could almost hear the music wafting from downstairs . . .

Brutally breaking into the dream came the reality of a horse's hoofs rapidly approaching the house. Emerald freed herself from Andrew's arms and stared numbly at Judah, who was hurling himself from his mount and charging the veranda like an enraged bull.

An almost contemptuous swipe of his hand knocked Andrew off balance and sent him sprawling.

'One man's wife not enough for you?' Judah grated, and then turned his attention to Emerald. She had never seen such black rage on a man's face before, and involuntarily she cringed away.

'Afraid, are you?' he snarled at her. 'You've reason to be! Come inside!'

He grabbed her arm in a savage hold and forced her to the door, half-dragging her to their bedroom, where he kicked the door shut behind them.

He gave her a searing look. 'You know damned well what I mean! I stopped you once from sneaking off to visit Standish, but how many other times have you met? How many times, while I've been away, has he divided his favours between you and my brother's wife?'

After everything she had already been through, this was the final straw. She slapped his cheek as hard as she could, and saw his eyes narrow, and the next moment he had pulled her towards him, his arms imprisoning her.

'Let me go, Judah!'

'The devil I will!' His laughter held an ugly sound. 'Why should I allow you to deny your legally wedded husband what you give so freely to Andrew Standish?'

As he spoke he was pushing her chin upwards, seeking her mouth. She fought desperately against what would clearly amount to a rough and brutal assault, an act of punishment for humiliating him in front of his enemy. But his arm was like a band of steel about her, holding her to him.

'I—detest you, Judah,' she panted. 'Let me go!'

'You may detest me as much as you choose! But by God, I'm going to break you in, woman, the way I would break in a horse!'

His lips were on hers, bruising in their intensity. And once again, to her bitter shame, her body turned traitor on her. He moved his mouth from hers, but he did not let her go.

'See?' The triumph was naked in his voice. 'I'm going to reduce you to the state where you'll crawl to my bed and beg me to take you! You may detest me, but I'm going to teach you to prefer my kisses to those of Andrew Standish!'

In her shame at the mounting desire inside her and the urge to respond to his touch, and also because she knew that he possessed the power to accomplish exactly what he had promised, she lashed out at him with her only weapon—words.

'*Never*, Judah! You, as a man, as a person, are utterly repellent to me! The only reason I cannot help responding to you is because I conditioned myself, a long time ago, to pretend that you are Andrew whenever you touch me! I knew it was the only way I could bring myself to suffer your attentions without being physically sick!'

He released her so suddenly that she almost lost her balance. The passionate rage had left his eyes, and in its place was something which reminded her fleetingly of a look she had seen in Timothy's eyes at times.

He slammed out of the room, and she flung herself face-down on the bed and wept for the death of her dreams and for the stark emptiness of the life which stretched before her.

Gradually she became calmer, and lay there wretchedly, thinking. How was she to face Claire again? Or Saul, for that matter? And how could she go on living with Judah in a state of loveless hostility, knowing that Andrew was so short a distance away? Andrew, who no longer loved or wanted her?

At last she rose, and washed her face and brushed her hair. Life had to go on, no matter how drearily. The children, as far as she was aware, were still in the barn, playing with the newborn kittens. They would have to be brought back to the house, to be washed in time for their supper and bed. But if she could possibly contrive it, she meant to avoid Claire and Saul, at least for the remainder of the day.

When she walked out on the veranda she saw that the children were there, talking to Judah. He looked up at her, his expression cold and hard, and she could see by the children's uneasiness that something in the atmosphere between herself and Judah had communicated itself to them. She searched desperately for a neutral topic of conversation, something with which to reassure them.

Before she could speak, Timothy said, 'Aunt Emerald and us found a dead sheep in a gully yesterday, Uncle Judah.'

He was instantly alert, his hard-muscled body tense. 'Where?'

'I'll show you, Uncle Judah!'

'No. You two go inside and get yourselves cleaned up before supper.' He turned to Emerald and said shortly, 'Show me the sheep.'

In silence she led Judah to the gully, and spoke only when they had reached it. 'I don't know why, but something made me order the convicts to cover it with canvas and stones, and keep it safe from predators.'

He merely grunted, and climbed down to the sheep. When he had removed the canvas weighted down with stones, she saw him pick up a stout stick lying near by and use it to turn the carcass over.

He replaced the canvas and levered himself out of the gully. He wore the look of a man who had received a blow below the belt.

'Is it—something bad?' Emerald ventured.

'As bad as it could possibly be,' he replied tonelessly. 'That ewe died of the scab.'

Inadequately, Emerald tried to offer consolation. 'It's only one sheep . . .'

'*You idiot*!' he snarled at her with a sudden, uncontrolled rage which she knew was not really directed at her at all. 'Scab is a vicious, and highly contagious disease which will sweep through the flocks like wildfire! And there's virtually nothing I could do to stop it!'

She remained silent, and watched him drop his head into his hands. He began to laugh without humour. 'Do you want to know the really ironical part of it all? If I'd known about this yesterday, I would have had all the sheep in the outlying runs moved far away from contagion, to safety. But a colonial regulation prohibits the moving of sheep from territory on which there is an outbreak of scab. Yesterday I would have flouted the law without batting an eyelid. Today—'

He shook his head, and continued bitterly— 'Today I was sworn in as a magistrate, committed to uphold the law. So I shall have to stand helplessly by and watch my flocks die.'

'I had an instinct,' Emerald exclaimed impulsively, 'that the death of the sheep was important! If only I had acted upon it, and insisted on the convicts searching you out immediately . . .'

'Yes.' He gave her a searing look. 'But I can always count on you to fail me somehow. Can't I, *dear wife*?'

CHAPTER SEVEN

THOSE UNFAIR, bitter words of Judah's drove a further wedge between them, and stopped Emerald from expressing the compassion which she could not help feeling for him as the virulent disease of scab spread through the sheep.

He worked like a demon to try and contain the outbreak. Water-tanks were filled with corrosive sublimate and the sheep dipped in this, but the scab was so highly contagious that it was a losing battle. When he was not helping his men to dip the sheep, Judah supervised the gathering up and burning of the dead carcasses. Water-holes which had become polluted by the disease had to be drained and filled in, and fresh water supplies made available to the surviving sheep.

Judah worked almost non-stop from early dawn until long after darkness; he would come in, wash off the accumulated grime and soot of the day, swallow the supper which had been kept hot for him and then stretch out on the sofa in their bedroom where he would fall instantly into exhausted sleep.

Now, it was Emerald who watched his unaware face at night by the light of a candle. He looked spent and gaunt, and even sleep did not wash the strain from his features.

But even in his preoccupation with the disease which was ravaging his flocks, he had not forgotten the promise he had made to Saul. Judah had set one of his convicts, who had been a cabinet-maker by trade before he fell foul of the law, to construct a wickerwork chair fitted with wheels taken from a child's bassinet. Saul quickly learnt to propel himself through the house, so that he was no longer trapped within the confines of one room, and Claire was also set free from her former almost constant vigil at her husband's bedside.

Emerald had felt tense and ill-at-ease with both of them since that emotionally shattering interview with Andrew, and in one way she was almost grateful for the outbreak of scab, for it provided a constant and safe topic of conversation between them.

Most of the time, doors and windows in the house had to be closed, in spite of the stifling heat, because the atmosphere outside was polluted by the stench of corruption and of burning flesh, the air alive with carrion birds flocking in to scavenge where they could before the fires claimed the carcasses.

One afternoon, overcome by the hot breathlessness inside the house, Claire fainted. Emerald quickly reassured the children and asked them and an anxious Saul to leave the room so that Claire could have such air as there was, and then applied her fan vigorously until Claire's eyes opened and she sat up with a muffled groan.

'*Oh God, how I hate this dreadful country!*' Coming from the usually serene and dignified Claire, the words had all the force of a string of obscenities.

Emerald had the feeling that, for the first time, she was glimpsing the real woman behind the mask. 'I had no notion that you felt like that . . .'

Claire pushed her heavy fair hair away from her forehead. 'I have been trained, from early childhood, to hide my feelings. I owed it to Saul to pretend. Only with Andrew was I able to share my dreadful homesickness, my loathing for all that is crude and coarse in this accursed place.' She gave Emerald a twisted smile. 'He told me that he was forced to admit the truth to you. You have been doing your own share of pretending, but I could sense your hostility and bitterness.'

'Why did you have to tell me that one devastating, unnecessary lie?' Emerald burst out. 'Why did you need to tell me that Andrew still loved me?'

Claire made a tired gesture. 'I thought it would comfort you. It was too late for it to make a difference; you were already married to Judah.'

'You have certainly been well taught to hide your true feelings!' Emerald lashed out bitterly. 'No one would doubt your devotion to Saul for a moment!'

'My devotion to Saul is real, Emerald. It is entirely possible to love one man passionately, and yet be concerned for the needs and the feelings of another.' A pleading note entered Claire's voice. 'Can't you understand my situation? I shall never have children of my own, never have a husband in the true sense of the word again!'

'What about me?' Emerald cried passionately. 'My dilemma is exactly the same as yours!'

'No, it isn't. You have a husband who loves you, and if only you could put Andrew from your mind . . .'

'*Judah* does not love me!' Emerald interrupted, staring at Claire.

'How blind you must be! Of course he loves you! It is patently obvious to everyone but you!'

Emerald looked at her in stunned silence. Could Claire possibly be right? She herself had never doubted that Judah desired her, but as for *love* . . .

The thought continued to preoccupy and tantalise her. It impelled her, a little later, to leave the house and go in search of him in order to test this startling new theory.

The land was scarred with great black patches left by previous fires, and by bleached bones from which the flesh had been plucked by predators that had beaten the fires.

Inside a dry creek two ewes, one obviously with lamb, were writhing on the ground in a most pitiful and demented way. They had scarcely any fleece left on their scarred bodies.

For the first time Emerald understood the awful reality of the disease. Before, the word 'scab' had been something abstract, something which caused Judah's sheep to die and the air to be polluted with the smell of burning carcasses, but now she understood the obscene manner of the animals' dying.

The disease caused an irritation which drove them almost insane, and they were trying to gain relief by rubbing their fleece off to the roots. And this same pitiful scene was being repeated over and over again in a hundred different places. Judah and his men faced the heart-breaking task of combing the land and collecting every single corpse for burning, and meanwhile they waited for other poor beasts to die in slow agony. Day after day after day . . .

She shuddered, and walked on in the direction of a pyre of carcasses being burnt. She almost choked as the smoke which hung like a loathsome pall over the scene entered her lungs. Holding her handkerchief to her face as a mask, she approached the fire and watched Judah as he supervised the burning.

Defeat was written on his face; his eyes were reddened by smoke and his face streaked with soot.

He saw her, and strode towards her. 'What do you want?' he demanded harshly.

Neither his expression nor his tone of voice indicated anything remotely resembling love.

'Nothing,' she answered curtly, angry with herself for having come on a foolish, impulsive mission. 'I just wanted to see what went on.'

'Makes a change, does it, from being cooped up inside the house?' Tension crackled in his voice. 'Well, there's a price to pay for relieving your boredom. Come on.'

He grabbed her arm and marched her back towards the house, but at one of the outbuildings he stopped. 'In here.'

'No! Let go of my arm, Judah! I don't . . .'

'I've no intention of risking contagion spreading to my prize ram!' he interrupted grimly. 'You have no interest in sheep, except in the dramatic spectacle of dead ones being burnt, so you won't have realised that I keep my prize ram tethered beside the house.'

'But what has that . . . ?'

'It only needs a piece of infected fleece adhering to your hair or clothing to be shed near the house, and carried by the wind or picked up by the shoes of anyone going to water the ram, and the animal for which I paid far more than I could afford would die in the same wretched way as the other sheep. So you will have to go through the ritual which I and my men go through nightly when we leave our tasks.'

Resisting, understanding nothing, she was forced inside the outbuilding. 'Take off your clothes,' Judah commanded.

'*No!*'

'Take them off! This is not some coy kind of game, Emerald! I'm fighting for the survival of at least some of my flocks! You and your clothes will have to be disinfected.'

She stared with horror at the large tank from which he was filling a pail. The smell of disinfectant was acrid in her nostrils. A shelf in the outbuilding, she realised, held stacks of spare breeches and shirts, and it struck her for the first time that when Judah returned to the house at night his clothes were always clean, in contrast with the soot and grime which streaked his face and arms.

She backed away from him. 'I'll be careful. I'll go straight home and wash my hair and bathe, and have the servants launder my clothes.'

'Your clothes will stay here until they have been thoroughly soaked in disinfectant.' His voice turned savage. 'I have work to do, woman! Stop wasting my time and get undressed!'

It was, she thought bitterly, the most humiliating thing which had ever happened to her, and somehow the most humiliating part of it all was that Judah remained totally unmoved and wooden as she stripped herself naked before his implacable gaze. Then he hurled the pail of stinging disinfectant solution over her head, and when she stood there, dripping and shivering before him, feeling utterly degraded, he flung her a towel and began to search through the clothing on the shelf while she dried herself.

He did not wait to see her dress in breeches of parramatta cloth and striped shirt, the uniform of a convict which was the nearest he had been able to find in her size, and a pair of boots far too large for her. Her own clothing had been thrown inside a large vat containing other male items of dress, and then he was off, back to his tasks.

Angry tears filled her eyes as she made her way to the house, hoping to gain it without being seen looking so utterly ridiculous and abased. But she almost collided with Saul's wheeled chair as soon as she entered.

'My dear Emerald . . .' he began in astonishment. His voice softened. 'You're crying!'

'Your—brother is a brute!' She dashed at the tears on her cheeks. 'I only wanted to see what he had to contend with—wanted to try and help.'

'You obviously *have* seen something of what he has to contend with,' Saul said gently, 'or he would not have forced you to go through the disinfecting process. Scab is a terrible thing, Emerald, and Judah is almost crazy with anxiety about that ram of his. He checks on it obsessively each day. It will break him if the ram gets the disease.'

She thought of the two ewes writhing in the gully, and shuddered, her own sense of humiliation put into perspective. 'Oh Saul, it's dreadful to see the poor beasts suffering so! Isn't there anything more Judah could do?'

'He is doing as much as he possibly can. To try and contain the disease, he won't allow direct contact between the home station and the outlying sheep runs. You may have noticed that Murphy drives out daily with a dray loaded with supplies and sheep-dip which he drops at various strategic points, to be collected by the farm constables. The quarantine Judah has imposed is so stringent that he doesn't even know, himself, how many of the sheep on other runs have been lost. That obviously adds to his mental torment.'

Saul sighed. 'We can only pray that enough of the outlying flocks will be saved so that Judah may start over again. But if he were to lose his prize ram—that would be a mortal blow.'

Emerald had a better understanding now of why Judah had treated her with such apparent brutality. As she hurried through the house to gain their room so that she could wash the stench of disinfectant from her hair and skin, and change out of the absurd breeches and shirt, she thought with compassion of the terrible difficulties with which he was coping.

The disease which scourged the sheep, the all-pervading stench of corruption and their enforced incarceration began to affect them all, even the children. Selina began to have nightmares, and she refused tearfully to be put to bed, terrified of the horrors which might invade her dreams. None of Claire's petting and comforting had any effect, and the battle to get her into bed at night was only won when Emerald said briskly, 'I'll magic the bad dreams so that they'll stay away.'

Selina looked desperately at her through her tears. 'Can—can you do that?'

'Certainly. Come on.'

Emerald made up an incantation which she

spoke solemnly over the little girl as the latter lay in bed, and perhaps because the children regarded her as their mentor and friend while Claire was normally the one who dealt out cuddles and kisses and words of comfort, Selina believed absolutely in the power of Emerald's 'magic'. Claire might tell soothing lies to calm their fears, but Emerald wouldn't, the children obviously reasoned.

After she had kissed them goodnight she heard Timothy say to his sister, 'Now you won't wake up in the night screaming, and wake me up as well.'

Emerald wished wryly that she had a similar incantation to believe in, to ward off her own restless dreams. Those dreams were no longer chiefly concerned with Andrew, as they used to be. They were jumbled, tortured images of Judah looking strained and tense, outlined against a burning pyre of sheep carcasses. Sometimes she dreamt disconcertingly of his arms about her, of his mouth tenderly upon hers, and then she would wake with a sense of yearning and stare in the darkness towards the sofa where he was sleeping off his exhaustion.

She was becoming more and more aware of him. She knew about the obsessive way in which he examined his prize ram each morning and evening, and she began to share his obsession.

To add to his troubles he was forced, from time to time, to leave his urgent and unwelcome duties on the station and preside over a case in the courthouse in his capacity of magistrate. Emerald could only guess at the frustration and despair which was building up inside him.

As the numbers of dead sheep increased and the

fires had to continue later and later into the night, so that Judah had to push the prize ram to the back of his mind, Emerald began to visit the animal instead to assure herself that it remained in good health.

Early one afternoon she was just returning from the part of the garden in which the animal was tethered when she saw that Andrew had arrived at the house. She greeted him abstractedly, only half-aware of his look of constraint and uneasiness. It seemed like a hundred years since their last meeting.

'I've come to see Saul, to report on the building work on their new house,' he explained in slightly embarrassed tones.

'I hope you came straight here, and didn't stray from the track!' she said sharply. 'We can't risk contagion reaching Judah's ram.'

'I made no detours. What is this about Judah's ram, Emerald?'

She explained briefly about the prize ram, and what its loss would mean to Judah. When she had finished, Andrew said with a frown, 'But why doesn't he move it to Saul's station? It would be completely safe from contagion there!'

'He can't. He is a magistrate, and it's against the law to move sheep from areas where there is scab . . .' She stopped, catching her breath.

She was not a magistrate. *She* had not sworn on oath to uphold the law in every respect. And here was one useful, practical service she could render Judah . . .

Aloud, she said, 'Will you do something for me? Will you help me to load the ram on your wagon, and allow me to go with you when you return, so that I may see the animal safely installed on Saul's station?'

Andrew hesitated. 'Well—Judah *is* a magistrate, and he already hates me. He could have me charged . . .'

'You need not be involved at all. I shall take full responsibility. Judah goes on working until late at night, and if we hurried you could bring me home again long before he comes in. I shall swear that I loaded the ram myself on to the trap and took it unaided to Saul's station. Judah may not believe me, but he wouldn't be able to prove otherwise.'

When Andrew still hesitated, she added deliberately, 'You do owe me something, I think—don't you?'

He flushed. 'Very well. I'll just go and have a quick word with Saul.'

With Murphy away delivering sheep-dip and supplies to outlying runs, and every spare man available helping with the searching out and burning of dead sheep, there was no one to see or stop Andrew and Emerald when they secured the ram inside the cage in which Judah had originally transported it from Port Phillip, and lifted it on to the back of Andrew's wagon.

While he drove, she steadied the ram's cage against the jolting of the wagon. It struck her, fleetingly, that she would never before in her wildest dreams have imagined a journey like this, with herself far too preoccupied with a prize ram even to spare Andrew more than a stray thought.

It was good to breathe sweet, clean air again as they approached Saul's station. The foundations for the new house had been laid, Emerald noticed, on higher ground, as Saul had promised Claire.

Also on high ground, temporary buildings had been put up for the convicts and servants and for Andrew's accommodation.

Emerald saw the ram safely installed in a paddock where it could graze and from which it couldn't stray, and while she was giving the overseer stern instructions about its care, Andrew had fresh horses hitched to the wagon.

They began the return journey in virtual silence. It came to Emerald all at once that it was not an awkward or embarrassed silence, or even an emotion-charged one. She and Andrew simply had nothing left to say to one another. Without her realising it, her passion and longing for him had burnt itself out.

They were about half-way home when one of the two horses suddenly stumbled over something on the track, and almost overturned the vehicle. Its partner neighed with angry panic. Andrew leapt from the dangerously tilting wagon to inspect the damage and Emerald scrambled down too.

It was obvious, even to her, that the horse had broken its leg. Grimly, Andrew freed it from the shaft and reached for his gun on the back of the wagon. He led the poor limping brute some distance away before he did what had to be done.

Emerald shuddered at the sound of the shot, and waited for him to return. She did not need to be told that they could not continue with one horse in the twin shaft.

'You'll have to ride back and fetch another.'

Andrew shook his head. 'This horse would not suffer a rider on its back. It has never been broken to the saddle. I shall have to walk back.'

'But it's miles!' she said with dismay.

'It can't be helped. You should be quite safe here on the wagon, but I'll leave my gun with you, just in case.'

She settled down to wait, gnawing the inside of her lip with anxiety. The sun dipped below the horizon, leaving a brief rosy glow in the sky before it began to darken. The stars appeared, shedding a ghostly light over the landscape, and the solitary horse dozed in its shaft. In the distance, dingoes howled.

Emerald clenched and unclenched her hands. Everything had gone disastrously wrong. Each moment she expected a tired and enraged Judah to come galloping up out of the darkness. He would have learnt from Saul that Andrew had called at the house, and he could not fail to associate her disappearance with that fact.

But no avenging hoof-beats approached. Perhaps, Emerald thought with a strange feeling of desolation, Judah was too tired, too indifferent to her to care where she was or with whom. Perhaps he had just fallen into bed, with no energy left to check on his prize ram, and consigned her to the devil. Claire had been utterly wrong when she'd said that Judah loved her . . .

When she did hear hoof-beats, long after midnight, it was Andrew bringing a spare horse which he quickly secured in the shaft. But even though he whipped up both animals unsparingly, dawn was streaking the sky by the time they arrived home.

Andrew dropped her and turned straight back. Emerald slipped inside the house, and encountered Alice coming from the kitchen.

'Why, madam, you're up early,' she said with surprise. 'I hope you have quite recovered from your sick headache.'

Emerald caught herself in time. She hadn't asked Andrew how much Saul and Claire knew, but one of them had obviously used the excuse of a sick headache to account for her absence from the dinner-table last night. As casually as she could, she asked, 'Has the master had his breakfast yet, Alice?'

'No, madam.' The housekeeper shook her head. 'He'll make himself ill if he continues like this. He has been working through the night, as you know, and he sent a couple of men over, a few minutes ago, to collect rations for breakfast. It seems they mean to go right on working without a break.'

So Judah had no suspicion of her activities, or even that she had been absent from the house. Hiding her relief, Emerald said, 'Perhaps I was foolish to rise so early. I'll just have a cup of tea in the kitchen, and then return to bed.'

Later, she was lying curled up on the bed, trying to decide on the most convincing story she could tell Judah to make him believe that she had, alone and unaided, taken his prize ram to Saul's station. She had still not made up her mind when she fell into an exhausted sleep.

She was brutally awakened by a hand on her shoulder, forcing her to sit upright. She stared into Judah's face, barely recognising him.

His hair was damp, and she could smell the faint odour of disinfectant still clinging to him. He had obviously just come in and bathed, and he hadn't even bothered to replace his shirt. There was a tautness about him, a hardness about his muscles which reminded her of a tightly coiled spring. But it was his eyes which frightened her most. They wore the look of a man pushed too far, a man who had gone beyond the limits of his endurance. He spoke in a dull monotone.

'I have just finished collecting and burning some two hundred sheep carcasses. I came home from that hell of destruction and death, hoping for a brief respite before I started again. And do you know what met me instead?'

'N-no,' she stammered, completely at a loss. 'If it's about your ram . . .'

'I've had no chance even to check on my ram.' His voice did not sound human; it was as though a machine were speaking to her. 'I washed under the pump, and I had just finished when Selina hurled herself at me, exhausted and weeping. She'd suffered nightmares during the night and had come looking for you, because it appears that you have magic ways of removing the horror from her dreams. And you were not here.'

'I—I was . . .'

'I know where you were!' Now his voice made her blood run cold. 'Selina knew too. She'd seen you going off with Andrew Standish. And you did not come back. All night.'

Emerald uttered a little cry of fear. 'Judah—no! You're mistaken! I did go with Andrew—but only to take your ram to safety on Saul's station—I knew you would not do so yourself . . .'

'*You lying trollop!* Since when have you cared about my sheep or my ram or about any of my hopes and dreams? All you've ever cared about was Andrew Standish!'

'Go—go and see for yourself! You'll find that

your ram is safely tethered on Saul's land, where no contagion can reach it . . .'

'Oh, I believe *that* part of your story! You needed an alibi, didn't you!' He jerked her towards him, his mouth coming down brutally and possessively upon hers. She began to struggle, beating at his chest, but it was like beating her hands against a stone wall.

His breathing was ragged and uneven when he moved his mouth from hers, and his eyes glittered with dangerous intensity. She felt his hands at the neck of her nightgown, ripping it to shreds, and when she tried to cover herself with the sheet he jerked it away, and snarled,

'Why such a display of false modesty, dear wife? You've allowed Andrew Standish to see you like this—kiss you—allowed his hands to fondle and touch you here—and here . . .'

In spite of her fear, in spite of the violence which consumed him, his hands sent a trail of fire burning through her.

'*Now it's my turn!*' he ground out.

She tried, while he was pulling off his breeches, to make her escape. Clutching the sheet to her, she had reached the door when he lunged at her, grabbing her roughly. As she struggled desperately with him, the sheet fell to the floor. She began to cry out, but he silenced her with his mouth on hers. Then he picked her up, still struggling, and threw her down upon the bed.

Her wrists were captured by one of his hands, her arms helplessly imprisoned above her head as he forced her thighs apart. The face above hers, the eyes which burnt into hers, seemed barely human.

Strangely, when he took possession of her, brutally and without tenderness, she no longer felt remotely afraid. She made herself submissive, willing herself not to cry out in pain and shock.

Instinctively, she sensed that if he had not had this violent release after all the agonies he had been suffering, and after his terrible rage at her, his strong spirit would have cracked. Recognising this, she ignored any feelings of humiliation and pain, and allowed her hands to move gently over his shoulders, even though he appeared to be oblivious of her submission.

When his rage and vengeful lust had been sated and her punishment was over, his arms remained locked about her, and she realised that he had fallen instantly asleep.

She also realised, with a great and unexpected tenderness, that he was weeping in his sleep like a small boy.

She lay quite still within his arms, murmuring soothing words of comfort and love which he could not hear, softly kissing his mouth, occasionally moving her hand to stroke his wet cheeks.

There was no question of her forgiving or not forgiving him. How could she blame him for believing that she had taken the first opportunity offered, the handiest excuse, to spend the night with Andrew?

She had never hidden her longing for Andrew; she had even told Judah that only by conditioning herself to imagine that *he* was Andrew could she bring herself to respond to his touch. And she had never given any sign of caring about Judah or his affairs.

Besides, if things had not happened in this way,

she might never have realised how deeply she had grown to love this husband of hers.

No, she could not blame him. All the same, it was ironical that her one and only attempt to help him had resulted in her being brutally violated by him.

CHAPTER EIGHT

JUDAH OPENED his eyes. For a moment they were clouded by confusion as he stared at Emerald's face so close to his own, and then she saw them darken with memory and bitter self-revulsion.

He drew away from her as though the touch of her had scorched him. He pulled on his clothes, and addressed a spot somewhere beyond her head.

'I'm . . . sorry,' he said thickly. 'I must have been insane . . .'

Don't apologise, she wanted to cry. *Come back, and take me in your arms, and kiss me, but with tenderness this time . . .*

Something about him rendered her mute. And then she understood. She might have forgiven him, but he could not forgive himself, and unfairly or not he was blaming her for having been the cause of his loss of self-control.

'Nothing like it will ever happen again,' he went on, his voice toneless now. 'You have my solemn oath on that.'

'Judah—I want to explain—about last night,' she began with difficulty. 'Andrew was driving me home when one of the horses broke its leg. He had to . . .'

'Don't insult my intelligence!' Judah interrupted rawly. 'I know what you're doing. You're desperately trying to save Standish's miserable neck with a pre-arranged excuse.' He gave a harsh, humourless laugh. 'You needn't fear, either of you. I have too much on my hands to waste time in wreaking revenge on him.'

'Please listen to me . . .'

'I have to get back to work.' He closed the door very deliberately behind him. There was a sound of cold finality about it. She would have felt better if he had slammed it.

She turned on her stomach and began to weep with reaction, with pain and a bitter sense of having lost something precious which had previously been within her grasp.

After a while she rose stiffly and painfully, and pulled on a robe. Then she rang for one of the maids to fill a tub with hot water, and bathed and dressed and arranged her hair with mechanical movements.

She had had nothing to eat since lunch-time the previous day, and yet she did not feel hungry. Her mind was a cauldron of different emotions, uppermost of which was despair. How could she reach Judah, and make him accept the truth?

I'll wait up for him tonight, no matter how late he might come in, she told herself. Somehow I'll have to break down the barriers between us.

The convict servant who arrived to clear up after Emerald's bath told her, 'Mrs Claire asked if you would join her and Mr Saul for tea, madam. They are having it early, because you missed lunch.'

She nodded, and made her way to the dining-room. Claire was arranging a tray on Saul's lap; he caught her hand in his and held it, and she dropped a kiss on his forehead.

Emerald's lips twisted. How innocent Claire, the true adulteress, appeared to the unknowing eye! Saul's total belief in his wife's love and fidelity could not have been in greater contrast to Judah's unfounded suspicions.

They became aware of her, and Saul exclaimed, 'We didn't know what to think when you failed to return home last night!'

Briefly Emerald described what had happened, and she noticed with bitter amusement that there was no hint of jealousy or disbelief in Claire's eyes. She was totally certain of Andrew's love and she had no doubts about the story Emerald was telling.

'By a stroke of luck Judah stayed out working all night,' was all Claire said. 'He came in for a brief rest and snatched a meal towards noon, but I dare say you were still asleep.'

Emerald made no comment. Saul remarked with a frown, 'I'm worried about him. I'd never seen him look like that before. He didn't even bother to check on his ram. It's almost as though he no longer cares . . .'

'He knows that the ram is safely on your station,' Emerald said tonelessly. 'I told him.'

'Oh! How did he take the news?'

She made a wry gesture, and said with heavy understatement, 'Much as you would have expected, I suppose.'

'He made no stupid threats to bring the animal back?'

'No.'

Claire changed the subject. 'There's something wrong with the children today,' she reported in a worried voice. 'I don't know what it is, and they won't tell me. Selina has been weeping for most of the day, and Timothy sulks. They've barely touched their food, too.' A hurt expression entered her eyes. 'They were quite rude to me when I tried to find out what was troubling them.'

Emerald set her cup down, glad of an excuse to get away. Saul was watching her with probing, puzzled eyes.

'Where are they? I'll go and see if I can discover what has upset them.'

'They're skulking in their room,' Claire told her.

Emerald knew precisely what was troubling the children, but she went through the motions of going to see them all the same. They were suffering from nothing more than lack of sleep. Selina's nightmares had obviously kept Timothy awake too, and that accounted for his ill-humour. What terrible damage those nightmares of Selina's had caused . . .

But when Emerald opened the door of their room she realised immediately that it was more than that. They stared at her in disbelief for a moment, and then they launched themselves at her like twin bullets.

'*You're back!*' Selina cried, and began to weep again.

Timothy, ashamed of his display of emotion, drew away from Emerald and began to scuff his shoes against the leg of the dresser. 'I thought you had left for good,' he muttered. 'Selina thought so too.'

Emerald looked at them, amazed. Because they had refused to discuss the matter with anyone, they hadn't been told that she had returned to the house that morning. But she would never have expected them to be so upset at the thought of her leaving them for good. After all, they had Claire.

'Would I really leave for good, without telling you and saying goodbye?' she chided. 'What put such a notion into your heads?'

Timothy gave the dresser a particularly vicious kick. 'We saw Mr Standish kissing you that day on the veranda, when you told us to go and play with the kittens in the barn. And then Uncle Judah came and knocked him down. We were peeping through the crack in the barn door, because we knew you'd only told us about the kittens to get rid of us. So we thought, Selina and I, that you had gone away to be with Mr Standish, now that Auntie Claire is here to look after us.'

Emerald shook her head, and decided not to rebuke them for having spied on her and Andrew. Instead, she pointed out, 'But you've always *wanted* your Auntie Claire to be the one to look after you!'

They said nothing for a moment, but looked at one another. Then Timothy offered gruffly, 'Auntie Claire—she . . . she hugs us too tightly.'

Emerald began to understand what the children were too young to formulate in their minds and express in words. Claire's love was cloying, possessive and stifling, and the children were beginning to feel smothered by it.

'She doesn't know about 'rithmetic,' Selina said lamely, trying to explain away an obvious conflict of loyalties. 'It's good for a person to learn about 'rithmetic and things.'

'Better than being hugged and kissed,' Timothy contributed eagerly, glad to be offered this excuse for their changed feelings.

Misty tears blurred Emerald's vision. When she could trust herself to speak, she said in a gentle voice, 'The best thing of all is to combine the two. I know how you feel about being hugged, Timothy, but would you mind if I did so now?'

'Only if you don't do it too tightly,' he conceded in an embarrassed voice, and moved into the circle of her arms.

She held the children to her for a moment, and then she let them go and sat down on one of the beds. 'Try not to hurt your Auntie Claire,' she said seriously. 'She can't help loving you too much. She thinks you were rude to her earlier today. Will you go and tell her you're sorry?'

A very adult sigh escaped Timothy. 'She'll want to hug and kiss us all the more, and make us sit on her lap while she tells us a story.'

Emerald interrupted, instilling a note of severity into her voice. 'There won't be time for that. I want you back in here within ten minutes. I'm going to teach you your letters.'

They grinned at her and left the room, and she stared unseeingly before her. How strange life was. She had won the children's love simply by giving up trying. If only she could persuade herself that the same tactics would work where Judah was concerned . . .

She dropped her face in her hands. *Tonight*, she thought. Tonight I must smash down the barriers between us. I must convince him that Andrew means nothing to me now.

The children returned, and she was forced to put the thought of Judah from her mind as she concentrated on teaching them to form the letters of the alphabet instead.

That night, after the rest of the household had retired, Emerald sat in the dining-room and waited for Judah to come home. He arrived much earlier than he had recently been doing, and long before she had expected him.

He checked when he saw her, and his face hardened. Then he shrugged and sat down and began to eat the cold supper which Alice had left out for him.

Emerald cleared her throat. 'You're early. I take it that is a good sign?'

'Do you?' His voice was expressionless. 'It merely means that almost all the sheep on the home station have now died and their carcasses are burnt. My men and I will have to start moving further afield, to lend a hand on other runs. I have little hope that enough flocks have survived for me to start again.'

She said nothing, for there was no comfort she could offer him. At last she broke the silence tentatively. 'Judah—about last night . . .'

'I don't want to hear about it,' he cut her short. His eyes were as cold and remote as those of a stranger. 'I've been doing a good deal of thinking, Emerald, and I can see that it was wrong of me to marry you in the first place. Well, it's too late to undo what has been done. The only solution is to make the best of things.'

'I am more than willing to make the best of things,' she began eagerly.

'Good.' His gaze rested on her for a moment. 'This is what we'll do. When the scab has run its course, I'll return my convicts to Government service, because there'll be little left for them to do here. I'll leave Murphy in charge of things, and I'll invest what money I can scrape together in a two-masted schooner, and I'll join the Mosquito Fleet.'

Her head was spinning. She moistened her lips. 'I don't understand what you mean. What is the Mosquito Fleet?'

'It's the name by which the many vessels which trade between Sydney and Broken Bay are known. I'll run up the salt-water creeks, carrying passengers and cargo.' He gave her an indifferent glance. 'I shall, of course, keep in touch with Murphy, and ensure that you do not go short of anything.'

She stared at him, appalled. 'You mean—you intend leaving? For good?'

'Yes.' There was no emotion in his voice. 'The children will go back to living with Saul and Claire . . .'

'No! What you are suggesting is—is abominable! All of it, but especially that the children should have their lives disrupted yet again! I suppose your implication is that I'm not morally fit to have charge of them!' Anger was making her lose sight of the whole objective which she had planned so carefully. 'Not long ago *Claire* was judged by you to be morally unfit!'

'I was wrong. I concede it now. All three of them—Claire, Saul, Andrew Standish—swore to me that the affair was over, that it had meant nothing, that Claire still loved my brother, just as Standish still loved the unknown girl in England who was waiting to marry him.'

He made a growling sound in his throat which could not possibly have been called laughter. 'I refused to believe them. But I've had the proof thrust under my nose so that I can no longer deny that it was true. Daily, I've watched the way in which Claire devotes herself utterly to Saul. I've seen his happiness, his sense of pride. And daily, I've witnessed your love-lorn longing for Standish which you did not trouble to hide as you held me at arm's length.'

His mouth twisted. 'You've told me, in so many words, that I repelled you, that I could never replace Standish as far as you were concerned. I caught you in his arms when you thought I was safely out of the way, and last night provided the final unanswerable proof.'

'You've got it all wrong! Nothing happened between us last night!'

'My dear Emerald,' he interrupted with harsh mockery. 'You are many things, but you are not a cold woman who places virtue above everything else! Even when you feared me, soon after we had first met, you could not help responding to me on the occasions when I touched you. And after you had conditioned yourself to imagine that I was Andrew Standish whenever I approached you— why, your responses became positively enthusiastic and even shamelessly abandoned!'

'Please . . .' she began, desperate to explain her lie, but he ignored her.

'So do not insult me by pretending that you spent the whole night alone in the company of the man you love, and who loves you, without any physical contact having taken place!'

She opened her mouth, and closed it again. He would never believe her if she told him the truth about Claire and Andrew. He had totally accepted Claire's unswerving devotion to Saul, and Judah was not a man who would ever be able to understand that, genuine though that devotion was,

Claire was also conducting a passionate illicit affair with Andrew at the same time.

No, Judah would be convinced that Emerald was trying to smear Claire in order to exonerate herself, and he would despise her all the more.

'So,' he went on, his voice implacable. 'I shall live on a schooner plying between Sydney and Broken Bay, and you will live here under Murphy's protection.'

'No! Please—you can't abandon me like that!'

'You are concerned about what people will say.' He shrugged. 'Yes, they will certainly talk, particularly as I expect that your association with Standish will go on flourishing. I can quite see that you would prefer the respectable illusion of my continuing presence, but it's a sacrifice I'm not prepared to make.'

He rose, and went on with chilly politeness, 'Now, if you will excuse me, I intend moving my things out of the room which we have been sharing so uneasily.'

'Please,' she whispered through bloodless lips. 'Don't do that . . .' Instinct told her that once he had taken that step she would never be able to reach him, never persuade him to change his mind.

She seized desperately on his own original reason for insisting that they should at least pretend to share a room. 'If you moved out, all the servants would know . . .'

He gave a crack of bitter laughter. 'I am long past caring about servants' gossip! But if you wish to retain a façade, you may tell everyone that I've moved out because my erratic hours were disturbing you. God knows, it will be a relief to abandon that damned uncomfortable sofa!'

She sat there for a long time after he had left her, staring unseeingly before her, tracing the design of the tablecloth without being conscious of what she was doing.

She had handled the whole situation wrongly. She ought to have put her arms about him, and told him that she loved him . . .

A long, dreary sigh escaped her. It would have been useless. He would have rebuffed her if she had tried to touch him, and his eyes would have darkened with contemptuous disbelief if she had told him that she loved him. He would have taken it for the desperate lie of a woman unable to contemplate being abandoned.

No, the root of the problem was that he had been fooled by Claire's devotion to Saul. Because it was so patently genuine, he now believed as firmly as his brother did that Claire cared only for her husband. And everything else followed from that.

At last she went to bed, and the candle-light showing the empty sofa brought an almost unbearable spasm of pain and loss to her heart. Somehow it symbolised the emptiness of her life from now on.

Almost imperceptibly at first, things began to change on the station. The smoke from the fires no longer hung over everything, for there were no sheep left alive and unburnt in the home pastures. Conceding defeat, Judah had relaxed quarantine restrictions; instead he and his men had saddled up, equipped themselves with bed-rolls and rations and billy-cans and were staying out on other runs to give such help as was needed there.

A ghost-like air hung over the homestead and its immediate surroundings. Now there were only the dairy cattle, a few pigs and the poultry left about the place, and two men had been left behind to care for them. Emerald could not help feeling that this was a foretaste of what she could expect for her future.

There was no one to whom she could confide the terrible desolation which filled her. Her friendship with Claire was not deep enough for confidences of that nature. Emerald could not even take comfort in the fact that the children had accepted her as the one by whom they wished to be cared for, because she knew that Judah had meant what he'd said—he would make them go back to Claire when the new house had been completed on Saul's station.

So, for the children's sake, Emerald was forced to distance herself from them, and she could see the perplexity and hurt in their eyes as she treated them with brisk and impersonal kindness.

Perversely, it only seemed to make them want to cling to her the more, and it caused her immeasurable pain to watch the lengths they were going to in order to win back her favour.

She dreaded Judah's return to the house, because she knew it would be no more than a preliminary to his leaving it for good, to live his own life on a schooner between Sydney and Broken Bay.

At night she cried herself to sleep as she contemplated the empty years ahead of her. She would not even have the consolation which Judah imagined— that of an illicit relationship with Andrew. She would be truly alone, with only convict servants for company. She would have to deny herself all but a few, token visits to Saul's station between long intervals, for the children must be given a chance to settle down with Claire again.

In the mornings Emerald felt too lethargic to get up, and she took to staying in bed until noon, ignoring the breakfast tray which Alice ordered to be brought to her by one of the servants. No doubt, because of this, she grew pale and hollow-eyed and never felt totally well.

It was Claire who opened her eyes to the truth. The two of them were sitting on the veranda one afternoon, busy at their sewing, when Claire asked suddenly, 'Does Judah know of your condition?'

'My—*condition*?'

Claire smiled, but there was such sorrow in her eyes that Emerald involuntarily caught her breath. 'I was expecting a baby at the time Saul was injured. Because of the shock, I lost it. But I remember the symptoms only too well to recognise them in you. Has it not occurred to you that that was the reason for your apathy and your lack of appetite in the mornings?'

Emerald put a hand to her face, totally amazed. She had thought she was suffering from simple unhappiness, but now that she added other, hitherto ignored signs, she knew immediately that Claire was right.

She said in a muffled voice, 'Judah does not know. Please don't mention it to anyone . . .'

'Of course not. But it will be something to cheer Judah after everything he has had to endure . . .'

Emerald made an incoherent excuse for going out, and began to walk aimlessly along the track leading from the house. After a while she sat down on a grassy knoll and stared out at the backdrop of shimmering blue mountains without seeing them.

The baby would make a difference. Surely the baby would change everything? Judah would not abandon her if he knew that she was carrying his child, no matter what his personal feelings for her might be. There was hope, after all . . .

Her hands went to her midriff, and she smiled. 'My baby,' she said aloud, with wonder. '*Our* baby, Judah's and mine . . .'

She felt transformed after that, as if she were walking on air. Saul commented on her glowing looks, and she and Claire exchanged secret glances; only the lurking background of sorrow in Claire's eyes momentarily dimmed her own happiness.

The day Judah finally came home, Emerald was on the veranda, sitting in the shade with the others. Saul was reading aloud to the children while the two women worked at their sewing. But this time both were engaged upon fashioning tiny lace-edged baby clothes instead of runners for table-tops or tray-covers as before.

The children first became aware of the cloud of dust on the horizon. They jumped up and down ecstatically as the dust began to resolve itself into a body of horsemen. Feeling sick with excitement, Emerald put her sewing away and waited.

As the horsemen approached, all three adults on the veranda became aware that this was not the homecoming they had been expecting and dreading, the return of men beaten and exhausted after a losing battle to save any of the flocks. There was an almost tangible air of exuberance about them, and as soon as they had reined in, Judah shouted to Murphy,

'Double rum rations all round for the men!'

He jumped from the saddle and took the veranda steps two at a time. 'We've done it! By God, we've done it!'

He grabbed Selina and swung her into the air, and when he set her down again he reached for Timothy, lifting the boy on to his shoulders. Judah's teeth were very white against the deep tan of his face as he laughed triumphantly. He turned to Saul.

'There were heavy losses on the nearest runs, which made me despair. While we coped with the searching out and burning, I ordered Murphy to send word to the various farm constables, telling them to muster their sheep and take a tally. I could scarcely believe it when the information had been gathered. The flocks on the outlying runs had totally escaped the scab, thanks to the rigid quarantine I imposed at the beginning! And there had not been one new victim for over a week!'

'Heaven be praised!' Saul said fervently.

Claire rose, and went to her husband. 'Come, my dearest, let us leave Emerald and Judah alone. Children, follow us. Your Aunt Emerald has something to say to your uncle.'

A pulse beat insistently in Emerald's throat. Claire had meant well, and of course she did not know about the deep trouble between the two of them, but Emerald would have preferred to choose her moment carefully before telling Judah about the baby.

He looked at her, and then glanced away, as if the sight of her caused him pain. 'Well?' he probed with stiff politeness.

She swallowed. 'I'm—so glad that many of your flocks have been saved. And with your ram healthy and strong, you will be able to start that new strain of high wool yielders you once told me about.'

'Fancy your remembering,' he interrupted sardonically. 'You showed no interest at the time, as I recall.'

She bit her lip, and looked steadily at him. 'What I am trying to say is this. You will now change your plans, and remain at Coorabee Creek to build up your flocks . . .'

'No. Murphy will be in charge. The only thing that has changed is the fact that my convicts will no longer need to be returned to Government service.' His voice hardened. 'And you, of course, will have more material comforts than I would have been able to supply merely by trading along the saltwater creeks.'

Emerald clasped her hands in her lap, and gazed down at them. 'Judah, you can't abandon me. I am expecting a baby.'

He remained quite still, and when she looked up at him her breath caught. His face was carved in stark lines, and his eyes were dark with rage and pain.

'So,' he snarled. 'You expect me to stay, and tacitly acknowledge Standish's bastard as my own!'

A blind mist formed before her eyes. She jumped up and hurled herself at him, dealing him a blow which sent his head rocking back. Then she gathered up her skirts and ran inside the house.

She was lying on her bed, sobbing, when she heard the door open and he came in. Pride forced her to sit up, to swallow her tears and compose herself as far as she was able.

He gripped one of the bed-posts, his knuckles showing white. She knew, by the bitter self-disgust written on his face, that he was remembering the last time the two of them had been together in this room.

He began to speak, his voice toneless. 'Because of what I did, I *do* have some responsibility towards you. You're right; I can't abandon you. So I'll change my plans. I'll stay here, and build up my new strain of sheep, and in public at least assume the role of father to your child.'

'You *are* its father, Judah!'

'Am I? How could I be sure? How could even *you* be sure?'

'I've told you—I've sworn to you . . .'

'My dear Emerald,' he cut in cynically, 'you have been lying to me from the moment we first met—remember?' He moved to the window, and stared outside. 'As I've said, I'll stay. I'll give your child my name, because there is at least a remote chance that he *might* be mine. But don't expect the impossible of me. Don't expect me to love the child, or to feel about it as if it were my own. Above all, don't expect anything to change between you and me.'

She was silent, stunned by the cold, hellish wasteland he had been depicting as the future which stretched before them.

He had been wrong about one thing. The situation between them *would* change—but for the worse. She would grow to hate him as she watched daily the way in which he slighted or ignored their child; she would not be able to stop herself from turning shrewish and hard, and their marriage would become a bitter battlefield in which each sought new ways in which to wound the other.

She clenched her hands together. To change that

appalling future, she would have to fight as she had never fought before. And she could not afford to care whom she had to hurt in the process.

CHAPTER NINE

JUDAH LEFT the room, and Emerald was still sitting there on the bed, trying to formulate her plans, when he returned with a stack of his clothes over his arm.

'You're moving back in here,' she said with a faint lifting of hope.

'There's nothing personal about it,' he replied tersely. 'I'm sharing the room with you for the sake of my own pride. Do you think I want the world at large to know that there is a question-mark over the parentage of the child which is to bear my name?'

She winced, but forced herself to try again. Almost inaudibly, she said, 'The sofa is uncomfortable. You admitted it yourself. I—would gladly share the bed with you . . .'

'Would you?' He gave a mirthless laugh. 'Pregnancy has changed you! It has made you more beautiful than ever, but also desperate. I wonder if you realise how insulting you are being, Emerald? You are offering me your body in the hope that you'll bind me so slavishly to you that I'll accept your child when the time comes for it to be born.'

'No . . .' she began painfully, but he went on as though she hadn't interrupted.

'If I'd been willing to play the game according to

your rules, your scheme might have worked. Much as I despise you for your treachery, I can't cultivate indifference to your physical charms. But I've sworn never to touch you again, so—I'll return to the sofa.'

A flush stained her cheeks. 'I don't know a great deal about these matters, but I would not have said you were a man who could contemplate a lifetime of celibacy . . .'

'I'm not, and I don't!' he assured her brutally.

Her flush deepened with anger and bitter jealousy. 'You mean . . . Surely you can't mean— you and *Alice*? I know she was your mistress once . . .'

'My dear Emerald,' he said in a hard voice. 'I have too much respect for Alice to discard her and then take her up again. Besides, you and I are to enact a charade of domestic bliss for the rest of our lives, aren't we? There will be other women, but my affairs will be conducted with discretion, and safely away from home.'

She jumped from the bed and went to the door, barely able to contain the revulsion of feeling which surged inside her. She would not be able to bear the future which he had spelled out to her. Each time he left Coorabee Creek, her sick fancies would imagine him with another woman, while she herself dragged through the empty days of her own existence.

She went in search of Claire and found her, as usual, ministering to Saul, making him comfortable by plumping up the pillows on his chair.

'May I speak to you in private, Claire?'

Saul smiled at Emerald. 'Women's talk!' he nodded indulgently. 'Claire has told me your wonderful secret, now that Judah has learnt it first. I'm so happy for both of you, my dear.'

'Thank you,' Emerald returned in a strained voice. Her response had been automatic; all her concentration was upon the battle in which she was about to engage. She was fighting for her future, her own and her child's.

Claire kissed Saul's cheek, and then went over to Emerald, who was trying to think of a sensible plan. Wherever they went, they were bound to be interrupted, if not by the children then by one of the servants. Making up her mind, she said for Saul's benefit, 'As a matter of fact, I wanted to consult you about the kind of things I shall need to buy for the baby. But why don't we drive to the township instead? Then you could advise me on what to buy.'

'Oh, by all means!' Claire agreed enthusiastically. 'There are several items I need from the store too, and I don't mind leaving Saul for a few hours, now that Judah is home.'

'You might get me some more laudanum while you're about it,' her husband said.

Claire pulled a disapproving face. 'I wish you would not take it, my love!'

'You know it is the only way I can get any sleep,' he reminded her defensively.

She sighed. 'Very well.' Turning to Emerald, Claire went on, 'We'll take the wagonette, shall we? I'm quite competent to drive it, and it is still early enough for us to get home again in plenty of time for supper.'

Emerald said little on the way to the township, but listened as Claire chatted on about the basic layette required for a first baby. She stifled a bitter laugh when Claire advised, 'You would do best to go for quality, so that whatever you buy may be passed on to future babies.'

But Emerald had decided to leave what she had to say to Claire until they were driving home again, and so she allowed the remark to pass.

This was the first time she had visited the township since her wedding day, and as she gazed upon the haphazardly scattered buildings, with the courthouse at its centre, her heart contracted with pain. What a fool she had been that day not to recognise the worth of the man who had given her his mother's favourite gown to wear for her wedding . . .

The store was a building of wooden slabs roofed with bark, housing a chaotic jumble of goods; casks of wines and spirits, tiered shelves displaying rolls of cotton prints and calico, tinware and ironmongery, groceries, cheese, spices, axe-heads and saws were all mixed up together in glorious confusion.

When they had selected some lengths of flannelette and of lawn, and Claire had made her own purchases, they began the journey home. But soon after they had left the township behind them, Emerald said quietly, 'Please rein in the horses, Claire. There is something I wish to say to you.'

Wearing a slightly puzzled frown, Claire obeyed, 'Is something worrying you?'

'Yes. Something is worrying me a great deal, to put it mildly.' Emerald's voice was blunt. 'Judah refuses to accept that the child I am expecting is his.'

'Good lord! But why?'

'He believes it is far more likely that Andrew is the father.'

Claire stared at her. 'What utter nonsense! Andrew would never . . .'

'You and I both know that,' Emerald interrupted pointedly. 'But Judah doesn't. He sees you daily, caring for Saul with devotion, and he believes the story all three of you told him—that the affair between you and Andrew meant nothing, that it is over, that you love only your husband.'

'Yes, I have realised by his changed attitude towards me . . .'

'Judah knows that I left with Andrew to take his prize ram to Saul's station, and that we didn't return until the next morning. He won't accept that absolutely nothing happened between us. He believes that we moved the ram solely to give ourselves an alibi, and that Andrew deliberately hitched an already lame horse to the wagonette for the return journey so that he would have to shoot it soon afterwards and thus give us an excuse for spending the night together. And nothing *I* can say will convince him otherwise.'

'I see . . .' Claire leant forward and patted her hand reassuringly. 'When the baby is born, he will put his suspicions behind him.'

'No, he won't. He has told me quite plainly what the future is to be. He will publicly acknowledge the child as his, but he will not regard it as his own, or love it. And he has sworn never to touch me again.'

'Oh dear . . .' Claire murmured inadequately.

'*You* are the only one who could convince him that his suspicions are quite unfounded,' Emerald said in a hard voice. 'You have only to tell him the truth—that your affair with Andrew is continuing in secret, that the two of you are in love to the exclusion of everyone else. You have explained to me with total conviction how it is possible for you to care devotedly for Saul while at the same time feeling passionately for Andrew. Explain it to Judah, too.'

'No,' Claire said softly but firmly.

'I am fighting for my future, Claire! I am fighting for the right of my child to be loved by its true father! You *have* to do as I ask!'

'No,' Claire said again. 'I can't. You have no right to ask me to deal Saul such a blow!'

'Saul need not be told. Speak to Judah in confidence.'

Claire gripped the whip she was holding so tightly that her knuckles showed white. 'Good God, Emerald, you know your husband by now! He is a man of strong feelings, and it's quite beyond him to dissemble! No matter how he might try, he would be totally incapable of hiding his contempt for me! And Saul would know—*he would know!* He would read it in Judah's eyes!'

'Saul accepted your affair with Andrew once; indeed, he engineered it. He would accept it again.'

'No! I won't do this to him!'

Emerald argued desperately, 'Would it be so very terrible if he knew? At least you and Andrew would be spared the need to be furtive about your affair. And when you measure it all against my whole future, and that of my child . . .'

'*You don't understand!*'

'No, I don't,' Emerald agreed frankly. 'You love Andrew, and I can quite see that you don't wish to hurt Saul unnecessarily.'

'It's not that simple! I love Andrew with passion, but what I feel for my husband is a great tenderness, a desire to protect him. He takes the place of the child I shall never have. And if he were to learn the truth now, after Andrew and I have succeeded in convincing him of our indifference to one another, it would be like—like giving a sweetmeat to a child, and when he has eaten it, telling him that it had contained poison!'

'I'm desperate, Claire!' Emerald said tensely. 'If you won't tell Judah, I shall have to do so myself!'

'I'll deny it.' Claire's voice was flat and hard. 'I'll make sure Andrew denies it too. There is no lie I would not stoop to in order to protect Saul. You would only do your case more harm by telling Judah about Andrew and me. He would regard it as desperate, spiteful slander.'

And she was perfectly right. Emerald brushed a hand across her brow. It seemed that she was beaten. For the moment she could not think of any further weapons with which to fight.

Claire whipped the horses up again, and they continued the journey in silence. Emerald broke it only once, when they were in sight of the house.

'I must warn you, Claire,' she said with a bravado she was far from feeling, 'that there is too much at stake for me to give up the battle. And if I have no other course but to do so, I shall fight dirty.'

'I take it that is a threat to tell Saul about Andrew and me, and persuade him to make Judah believe it too.' Claire's voice was hostile now. 'Try it, Emerald, and I'll swear on the Bible if need be that it's a lie!'

'You won't have to perjure yourself before the Almighty,' Emerald said shortly. 'If Saul is to learn the truth, he must learn it from you. I shall say nothing to him about it.'

But the next morning she found herself hard put to it *not* to confide in Saul. He wheeled himself out to the veranda, where she was staring blankly into the distance, and said gently, 'My dear Emerald, what is the matter?'

She looked at him, and saw the warmth and compassion and wisdom in his eyes. 'Nothing,' she lied, and tried to smile.

'That is patently not true. There is an air of such desperate sadness about you, and as for Judah . . .' Saul shook his head. 'I watch him whenever he is unaware of it. He reminds me of the way he had looked when our mother died suddenly. *Bereft*. That is the only word for it. Why should he look as if someone he'd loved dearly had died, when he has all the reason in the world for rejoicing? Not only has he beaten the scourge of scab, but he is to become a father. He . . .'

'You are imagining it all,' Emerald interrupted, her voice muffled, and fled.

But her feelings were to be harrowed even further, for when she escaped into the bedroom she found Timothy and Selina there, sitting together in an armchair and clearly determined to wait until they could speak to her alone.

Timothy stood up, and cleared his throat. 'Selina and me have come to ask you why you don't like us any more.'

'But I do!'

'No, you don't,' he contradicted flatly. 'You leave us with Alice, and you don't give us lessons any more. And when Selina and me went out early this morning, and picked some flowers for you and put them by your plate at breakfast, you didn't even look at them.'

She had seen the flowers, stiffly stuck inside an old medicine bottle, and a lump had formed in her throat. But she had deliberately ignored them and hadn't caught the children's eyes.

'I—didn't know they were for me,' she lied lamely. 'I thought you'd decided to brighten up the breakfast-table. I'm sorry.'

'You're not telling the truth, and you're not a bit sorry,' Timothy accused. 'You stopped liking us a long time ago. We just wanted to come and tell you that we don't *care*!' His voice broke on the last word, belying his aggressive statement, and Selina was openly weeping as they ran from the room together.

Emerald sank on to the bed and dropped her face in her hands. It was too bitterly unfair that the children should also be casualties of the desolate chasm which existed between herself and Judah. They, at least, would have to be saved.

Making up her mind, she changed into her riding habit and rode out into the paddock where Judah was in charge of drafting selected ewes for crossbreeding with his prize ram. He saw her, and came to join her when she dismounted. His face was an expressionless mask.

'I need to speak to you,' she said. 'I've deliberately been putting a distance between myself and the two children since you told me that they would be sent back to live with Claire. They feel it very much. They have become attached to me, and I to them. You must allow them to remain with us. Don't punish them also, Judah.'

'It is not to *punish* them that I intend sending them back to Claire.' His voice roughened. 'It's for their own good. Children are sensitive to atmosphere. What kind of atmosphere do you imagine will prevail here in the years to come? I, too, am fond of the children, and I shall miss them very much. I'll miss them more than you will, for I've no doubt that you will become completely wrapped up in your child after it has been born.'

She turned away, numbed by his coldness, by his pointed reference to *her* child, and by his reminder that there would never be any joy or happiness or lightness of spirit on Coorabee Creek again. He was right; its poisoned atmosphere would not be one in which to bring up children, and she thought with desolation of the future of her own unborn child.

As she rode back to the house, the glimmering of an idea came to her and she worked on it, ruthlessly polishing it in her mind until she had perfected it.

Claire flatly refused to tell Judah the truth about herself and Andrew. So there was only one possible thing to do. Emerald would have to trap her and Andrew into giving themselves away.

But the timing would be important. Saul must not be present to witness his wife's denunciation. That was something he would have to be spared. Emerald began to watch, to make mental notes and to formulate her plan.

In the evenings, after supper, Saul would habitually remain for a while in the living-room with the others, making conversation. Then he would ring for the two male convicts who had been given the duty of lifting him out of his chair and into bed. He always said goodnight to everyone before he wheeled himself out of the room, accompanied by the convicts.

He disliked Claire witnessing the awkward manoeuvring to transfer his helpless body into bed, and so she always kissed him tenderly before he left the room, regularly adding a plea that he should try to sleep without the aid of laudanum. Just as regularly, he promised to try to give up the habit.

Emerald took careful note of the times he retired, and secretly looked into his room on a couple of occasions after he had left them. He was in bed by half past eight, and fast asleep on both the nights she checked, so she knew that he continued to rely on laudanum in spite of his promise to Claire.

The public unmasking of Claire would have to take place between half-past eight and nine o'clock at night, therefore, when the children would be safely in bed, Saul in a drugged sleep, and Judah making a public show of keeping the two women company in the living-room before he disappeared into his office. Once shut up there, he invariably worked on his accounts until late into the night, so that he could be certain Emerald would be asleep before he entered their room. So everything would have to be dovetailed to fit into that vital half-hour.

There were one or two obstacles which seemed to her to be insuperable. She was poring over them as usual during breakfast one morning when Judah came in from outside, late for the meal.

'I'll ask Hettie to cook something fresh for you,' Emerald told him with the polite consideration which they now adopted towards one another in public.

'It doesn't matter,' he returned, and sat down to pour himself a cup of tea. He looked abstracted.

'Is anything wrong?' Saul wanted to know.

Judah frowned. 'Murphy went out yesterday afternoon with rations for the convicts on the north-east run, and he hasn't returned. I don't know what the devil could have happened to him.' He pushed his empty cup aside and stood up again, moving restlessly to the open window. Emerald saw him tense.

'Can any of you smell something?' he demanded, turning.

'Only ham and eggs . . .' Claire began.

'Let's go out to the veranda.' He strode from the room, and the rest of them left their breakfast and followed him.

'Can you smell it now?' Judah demanded.

Emerald caught a very faint whiff of eucalpytus, pungent as incense, borne upon the wind. But before she could mention it, or ask about its significance, furious hoof-beats approached the house and a moment later Murphy half-jumped, half-fell, out of the saddle. He came towards them in a weary, shuffling run and clung to one of the veranda posts for support.

'Sor,' he addressed Judah hoarsely. 'The convicts, sor—Every man-jack of 'em . . .'

In spite of his visible air of tension, Judah said, 'Get your breath back first. Timothy, run back to the breakfast-table and fetch the pitcher of milk.'

When the overseer had drained the pitcher in large gulps, he was able to go on more coherently, and they all listened in grim silence as he told his story.

When he'd arrived at the north-east run the previous afternoon, he had found the farm constable unconscious and tied up, and all the convicts gone. They had taken with them the constable's weapons and had also armed themselves with picks and shovels.

Murphy had ridden to the next run, and the next. The same situation had met him at each.

'The convicts is a-firin' the forest in the foothills, sor, and they means to march on the house when they're t'rough! There's murder in their hearts, sor, so there is . . .' His eyes rolled with fear.

'All right, Murphy, that will do!' Judah interrupted tersely. He looked around him. 'Get inside the house, and *stay* inside, everyone. Shutter all windows and make certain that there is a plentiful supply of water to hand, just in case.'

All but Emerald obeyed him. Once she had seen the children safely in Alice's charge, she returned to the veranda where Judah was questioning the overseer more closely. She interrupted, forgetting the strain and tension between them, her voice anxious.

'Will your flocks be caught up in the fire if it spreads from the foothills?'

Judah's reply was mechanical. 'No. The pastures are too green and treeless to burn. But the forest fire is still a serious matter, because we rely heavily on the timber. And the wild animals which escape the fire will compete with the sheep for grass. More seriously, the forest is the traditional hunting-ground of the nomadic Aborigines, and if they return and find it destroyed, they'll take revenge by attacking us.'

He added trenchantly, 'Now do as I said, and get inside the house!'

The next moment he was loping towards the outbuildings with Murphy in tow. Ignoring his command, Emerald followed, and heard Judah call the home station convicts together. She stared at the horizon, but there was nothing to show that the forest beyond it was on fire. Only that unmistakable smell which was borne upon the wind, and which she now realised was the scent of burning eucalyptus, confirmed Murphy's story.

She heard Judah addressing the convicts, ordering them to saddle up, to arm themselves with whatever they could find, and ride out with him to quell the riot. They stood stolidly, unresponsively, before him, and made no move to obey.

He swore at them roughly. 'Do you want your tickets taken away? And those of you who have not yet earned your tickets—do you want extra service added to your sentence? *Do as I say!*'

' 'Tis our own kind out there, sir,' one of them mumbled. 'You can't rightly ask us to turn on them.'

They remained deaf to all his other threats and pleas. At last he conceded defeat. 'Well, will you at least help me to fire a circle around the house and outbuildings, to protect them, or do you choose to martyr yourselves by being burnt alive with the rest of us? Your friends out there mean to turn their attention on us when they've finished destroying the timber!'

The convicts hastily signalled their agreement and dispersed. Emerald touched Judah's arm. 'Couldn't you organise your neighbours to help you put down the riot and save the timber?'

'There wouldn't be time. The neighbours are too scattered.' He added roughly, 'Get back to the house!' Then he strode away to supervise the convicts.

Armed with wet sacks and pails of water, the convicts set fire to the scrub surrounding the house and outbuildings in a wide circle, controlling its spread with the wet sacks. Although it was a totally unfamiliar sight she was watching, Emerald understood what they were doing. Any fires the rioting convicts might set nearer the house as they advanced would be unable to leap the fire-break.

Strangely, it did not occur to her to fear for her own safety, or for that of the rest of the household. Instead her thoughts went out to the convicts who were bent on this senseless destruction. Surely they must realise that they were were bringing doom upon their own heads? The mere fact that they had armed themselves with guns stolen from the farm constables carried with it a sentence of death. Something very drastic must have happened to drive them to this desperate act . . .

She had a sudden mental image of Nat Williams, the convict she had found penned inside a hut, on the verge of starvation. She remembered how he had told her of the brutality of the farm constables, and the corruption which they practised. And she also remembered him saying to her, *'If ever Nat Williams can be of service to you . . .'*

Instantly making up her mind, she hurried to the stables and saddled her horse. Then, gathering up her skirts, she mounted and began to ride furiously, digging her heels into the flanks of the gelding to spur it into jumping the strip of smouldering earth created by the fire-break. She heard Judah shouting to her to come back, but she ignored him and spared neither herself nor her horse as she galloped in the direction of the foothills.

She became aware that Judah was following her, and then he had gained upon her on his more powerful stallion.

'Are you crazy?' he shouted, leaning across and grabbing at the reins in her hands, forcing her gelding to slacken its pace and then come to a halt. 'What do you think you could accomplish? And galloping at breakneck speed in your condition, too!'

'*My condition, Judah?*' she echoed bitterly. 'Why should that cause you any anxiety? Do you think I haven't guessed how many times you must have prayed secretly that I might lose the baby you refuse to believe is yours, so that you may be free to go and live on a schooner between Sydney and Broken Bay?'

He looked away, and didn't answer her accusation or deny it. After a pause he merely repeated, 'What do you think you could possibly accomplish against a mob of rioting convicts?'

'I am the only one, Judah, who may conceivably save the timber forest for you. Now kindly let go of my reins. Whether you decide to accompany me or not is entirely your own affair.'

'You are to return to the house immediately!' He threw the reins back at her. 'Do you hear me?'

She spurred the gelding on instead, and cried over her shoulder, her voice catching, 'Who knows, Judah—you may be lucky! The convicts may shoot me on sight, and then you'll be free of me for ever!'

CHAPTER TEN

Perhaps because he recognised the grim purpose which was driving her on, Judah made no further attempts to persuade or force her to return home, but rode beside her. His voice reached her in ragged snatches, carried by the wind which their own speed created.

'Will you tell me—for the love of God—what you are hoping for?'

'There's a convict,' she shouted back, 'who owes me a favour, and who may be prepared to listen to reason.'

The sun beat remorselessly down upon them, and now they could smell the smoke from the foothills and see it blackening the sky in the distance. After a while, above the pounding of their hoof-beats rose a sound like roaring thunder. Now they could feel the hot blast of the flames competing with the intensity of the sun.

But when the smoke cleared momentarily they could see that, as yet, only a relatively small part of the forest had been destroyed. There was still time to appeal to the convicts, time to save the majority of the eucalyptus trees and the undergrowth which sheltered the animals regarded by the Aborigines as their legitimate prey.

Judah and Emerald could now pick out individual figures of convicts, silhouetted against the leaping orange flames.

They, in turn, had been spotted, and the convicts began to surge forward, something satanic about them as they advanced, their faces blackened by smoke and brandishing their weapons.

With a kind of unreal fascination, and recalling her own bitterly mocking words, Emerald watched as one of the convicts dropped the butt of his stolen fowling-piece on the ground, rammed down the powder and placed a ball in the muzzle. In another few moments he would be ready to take aim and fire.

'Fall behind!' she shouted urgently to Judah. 'I stand a better chance on my own! Join me when I have made contact with Nat Williams!'

'No! Get behind cover . . .'

'It's the only way!' She was streaking ahead even as she spoke, holding the reins in one hand, waving her white handkerchief in the other. That, together with the fact that she was now clearly recognisable as a female, must have persuaded the man with the fowling-piece to hold his fire.

'Let me speak to Nat Williams, please!' she cried.

'Blood and 'ounds!' one of the convicts shouted. ''Tis the little lady what took the whip to Jem Connors!'

She slid from her horse and, as she did so, Judah reached her side. He addressed the men. 'Why in the name of heaven are you doing this? Can't you see that it could mean a death sentence for every single one of you?'

'What odds?' a convict cried with searing bitterness. ''Tis a livin' death we're leadin' anyhow!'

Emerald saw a man shoulder his way towards the front, and recognised him as Nat Williams. 'Good day, ma'am,' he said stiffly. 'I reckon I owe you for what you did for me that day, back in the hut. But you went back on your promise, didn't you? Nothing changed. You did not tell your husband of our conditions, as you said you would . . .'

'She did tell me,' Judah interrupted. 'But I decided she was exaggerating in her ignorance of conditions in the colony. And when I went round the runs myself to enquire into the matter, I received no complaints.'

'Of course you didn't, sir,' Nat Williams said sourly. 'You asked your questions in the hearing of the farm constables, who'd had advance warning of your coming and who made sure you would find no evidence of what had been going on. Everyone was too afraid of reprisals to convince you of the truth.'

'Then let me hear now from your own lips what has been happening to inspire this act of lunacy!' Judah commanded.

By tacit consent, the convicts allowed Nat Williams to be their spokesman. 'What has been happening, sir, is graft and corruption practised by the farm constables and your overseer, Murphy.'

'*Murphy!*' Judah echoed in disbelief.

'Indeed, sir,' Williams insisted grimly. 'Murphy was in charge of distributing rations to the runs. What he did was to leave only enough rations to last until Thursday each week. So from then until late on Saturday night, when he arrived with more rations, the convicts on our particular run starved. The same thing happened on the other runs—we were all kept on short rations. If we dared to complain, the farm constables flogged us. They and Murphy were sharing between them the money saved by keeping us half-starved.'

Judah shook his head. 'I trusted Murphy absolutely. He has been with me for years . . .'

Nat Williams was forced to pause in his indictment, for the heat from the burning timber was so intense now that they all had to move further away. He continued,

'And then, sir, two poor wretches among us died of overwork and malnutrition. We have a secret system of communication between the different runs, sir, and we all knew what had happened. We thought that at last the truth would come out. You, as a magistrate and owner of the land, would have to be informed of the deaths, and you could not have failed to see why the men had died.'

His voice took on a harsh note. 'Instead, sir, Murphy told the two farm constables in charge to fire shots into the bodies of the dead men, and to move the bodies a long way away, so that when they were eventually found it would seem that they had escaped and become bushrangers, and fallen foul of bounty-hunters or other rival bushrangers. We knew, then, that we could hope for no help from anyone but ourselves. We made our plans, and we acted simultaneously to overwhelm our farm constables and arm ourselves with their weapons. Then we made for the forest.'

The wind changed momentarily, forcing the fire back upon itself, so that it gave renewed attention to previously half-burnt tree-trunks.

Judah asked helplessly, 'What did you all hope to achieve by firing the timber?'

'Before we knocked the farm constables senseless, sir, we told them that we meant to burn down the forest and then march upon the house. It was a bluff, sir. We knew Murphy would find the constables and learn from them of our threat. We reckoned on you coming hot-foot after us, so that we could put our case before you. If we had marched on the house, it would have constituted a riot in the eyes of the law, so we chose this way instead.'

Nat Williams gestured ruefully towards the fire. 'We'd meant to burn down only one or two trees. But a sudden wind sprang up, and it all got out of hand, as you can see.'

Judah thought rapidly. 'If you'll throw down your weapons, and help to fight the fire, I'll give you my word on two things—Murphy will be punished, and the farm constables replaced by men whom I'll vet personally and keep a strict eye upon. In addition, the action you have taken will be disregarded, and no punishment meted out. What do you say?'

'And how are we to fight the fire, sir?' Williams asked sardonically. 'Scoop up water from one of the streams with our bare hands, and sprinkle it on the flames?'

'Of course not,' Judah snapped. 'I'll have to ride back for help and a plentiful supply of sacks.'

'Forgive me, sir,' Nat Williams returned quietly, 'but I'm thinking you'll come back, not only with sacks and helping hands to fight the fire, but also with dragoons to arrest us. Even though we did not mean to, we have caused you a great deal of damage, and I cannot see you overlooking it.'

'I give you my word . . .' Judah began.

'No, sir, I'm sorry. Our very lives are at stake. As

you pointed out yourself, each one of us could be sentenced to death for what we have done.'

Judah swore under his breath. With a thrill of fear, Emerald saw that those convicts who bore firearms had ranged themselves on either side of Nat Williams.

'Just what do you propose to do?' Judah demanded.

'Well, sir, we're desperate, as you can see. We want your horses, so that you and the lady won't be able to reach help in time to stop us, and then we'll take our chances in the bush.'

'I give you my solemn oath,' Judah said forcefully, 'that dragoons will not be brought into the matter! If you'll allow my wife and me to return for home . . .'

'I don't believe, sir,' Williams interrupted with cynical bitterness, 'that a gentleman like yourself would regard an oath sworn to *convicts* as solemn! There is only one condition under which we would allow you to go for help. Leave your wife here with us as a mark of good faith, in the knowledge that at the first glimpse of a dragoon's uniform she will be shot.'

'*No!*' Judah thundered.

'Yes,' Emerald amended, quietly but with determination. She turned to Judah. 'It really is the only way, and I'm not afraid of the convicts. It wouldn't be in their interests to harm me.'

He stared at her, and she could almost see the struggle taking place in his mind. At last he addressed Nat Williams. 'Very well,' he said curtly. 'But I make one condition. There's a stream not far from here. I want my wife kept there so that she'll be safe from the fire if the wind should change.'

Williams nodded. After Judah had watched half a dozen armed convicts escorting Emerald to the stream, he galloped away as fast as his powerful stallion could carry him.

One of the convicts guarding Emerald, a young man barely out of his teens, approached her and said shyly, 'I reckon you don't remember me, ma'am. 'Twas me you saved from Jem Connors's whip that day. I'm Rob Stapleton.'

'You have a fine way of showing your gratitude,' Emerald returned drily, glancing at the carbine in his hand.

He blushed to the roots of his hair, and mumbled, 'Sorry about this, ma'am. We agreed to let Nat Williams take charge. I—I wanted to tell you, ma'am. I'd do *anything* for you.'

'Thank you,' she said, more gently now, and was suddenly struck by a thought. 'There *is* something you can do—for me, for all of us! Go and give Nat Williams a message. Instead of standing around uselessly, watching the fire spreading, the convicts could be creating a fire-break to contain it. They could take off their shirts and soak them in the steam, and use them to control the flames.'

Soon she had the satisfaction of seeing them do just that. She sat by the stream, ignoring the armed convicts who were guarding her, and from time to time splashed water over her face and hair to combat the fierce heat of the fire.

The air was filled with the roaring of the flames fed by the wind. The feeble sunlight which struggled through the smoke cast an unearthly gloomy purple glare over everything. Where the fire had swept triumphantly on its destructive path, blackened skeletons of trees stood stark and forlorn, marking the desolate landscape.

Judah returned, accompanied by the home station convicts and a plentiful supply of sacks. Only now did the convicts relax their guard over Emerald and throw aside their weapons, and hurry to help fight the fire.

Judah relaxed visibly when he saw that she was unharmed, but he made no move to touch her. All he said was, 'You must go home. I don't like to think of you riding all that way alone, but I *have* to stay here, in control.'

'I know,' she interrupted. 'There's a young man among the convicts—Rob Stapleton—he is entirely to be trusted. Let him ride back with me.'

Judah nodded, and called to the nearest convicts to find Rob Stapleton. While they waited, Judah reported grimly, 'Murphy lost no time in taking to his heels. He knew the game was up. But he'll be caught and made to stand trial.'

She looked into his eyes. 'Judah—I told you the truth about the conditions your convicts were enduring. You didn't believe me at the time. Doesn't it occur to you that you might be equally wrong about my baby?'

Raw pain entered his eyes. 'Do you think I don't *want* to believe you?' he demanded hoarsely. 'Do you think I haven't, time and again, tried to convince myself that you are to be the mother of my child, so that the past might be wiped out and we can start afresh?'

He shook his head. 'I *can't*, Emerald! I've never been able to pretend to myself, and I can't pretend that you don't have the most powerful motive for lying. A woman will do anything, say anything, to protect her own young. Take gentle Alice, for example. She endured beating after beating from her husband, and it was only when her unborn child was threatened that she went to the extreme of stabbing him.'

There was no answer which Emerald could possibly have offered to that statement.

A muscle jerked beside Judah's mouth, and he looked away from her. 'There is one other matter which I have never mentioned before, and which I mention now only with the greatest reluctance. When I—when I raped you—you did not cry out in pain, and I have been haunted by the memory that you actually responded to some extent. Those were not the reactions of a virgin, Emerald.'

How could she possibly have explained to him, in a manner which he would have accepted as true and convincing, her own complex motives and feelings at the time? She remained mute, as he went on in a heavy voice, 'So they will always be there between us, my doubts and suspicions.'

No, they won't, she vowed silently. The time had come to put her plan into action, and the drama of the revolt among the convicts had given her the excuse she had been needing. It had also solved one other problem for her—the question of an absolutely trustworthy messenger and co-conspirator.

Rob Stapleton was approaching, leading a borrowed horse and Emerald's gelding. She addressed Judah, apparently changing the subject. 'Could Rob be allowed to remain at the home station? I want to teach him to groom and exercise my horse.'

'My dear Emerald,' Judah said with a wry smile.

'I owe you far, far more than just the granting of that simple request. Yes, of course.'

He helped her into the saddle, and then hurried away to direct the fight against the fire.

It was late afternoon by the time Emerald and Rob Stapleton reached home. Gratefully, she bathed and ate the substantial tea which Alice ordered to be served to her in the bedroom, and afterwards went straight to bed where she fell asleep immediately, exhausted by the exertions and the drama of the day.

Almost twenty-four hours after it had first raged out of control, the fire was finally beaten. Judah and the home station convicts returned towards noon the following day, exhausted, their faces blackened by smoke and their hair singed by the flames. Judah washed and ate and then slept for an hour before he was up and about again, supervising the allocation of generous rations to the convicts, vetting potential farm constables and arranging for the former ones to be arrested.

In their bedroom, Emerald was busy too, working out the timetable for her plan. Tonight she would be putting it into operation. She sat by the dressing-table and took up a pen, and thought for a moment, deciding on the wording of the note which she meant to ask Rob Stapleton to deliver for her in secret.

After a while she began to write in a hasty scrawl, as if driven by great urgency and agitation.

'Andrew—a most terrible occurrence—Our convicts went on the rampage. Claire was among those injured—I know you would want to be told. In haste—E.'

She re-read the note several times, slowly. Its

contents would send Andrew, half-crazed with anxiety, to come and find out the extent of Claire's injuries. The two of them could not help giving themselves away in the presence of Judah . . .

Emerald shook her head, and her shoulders slumped. *I can't do it,* she thought hopelessly. *I can't crucify Andrew like this. I can't strip Claire naked* . . .

Tears blurred her vision as she held the note to the candle which she had lit with the intention of using its wax to seal the note. She watched it being reduced to ashes, and knew herself to be finally beaten. The plan upon which she had expended so much energy, thought and hope was one which she could not bring herself to carry out.

She blew out the candle and went to the veranda. Dusk was tinging the sky with faint colour, and somewhere out there among the outbuildings Judah was still working. Tonight he would be seeking the uncomfortable sofa again, and tomorrow night, and all the nights for the rest of their lives . . .

A sound behind her made her turn, and she saw that Saul had wheeled himself out of the house. 'Emerald,' he said quietly. 'Please tell me what is wrong.'

She forced a smile. 'Nothing whatsoever is wrong!'

'My dear girl, you performed the most heroic act yesterday by riding out to face the convicts; you willingly allowed them to use you as a hostage. Because of your actions, a nasty situation was averted, and Judah was able to save most of the timber. And today he came home, the fire beaten, and instead of sweeping you into his arms and demonstrating his gratitude and his love and his concern for your condition, he merely pecked you politely on the cheek! And you expect me to believe that all is well between you!'

She said nothing but stared blindly before her, her lower lip caught between her teeth. She heard Saul sigh. 'Since you won't confide in me, I'll tell you what I believe to be the trouble. Judah suspects that the baby you are carrying is not his, but Andrew's.'

She made a startled sound, and Saul went on wryly, 'I'm not a fool, you know. I remember the night you were forced to spend with Andrew, and I realise that Judah must have found out about it. Am I right?'

'Yes,' she admitted, almost inaudibly.

Saul shook his head. 'In Judah's shoes, I would have smothered my doubts and suspicions and forced myself to believe that the child was my own. But Judah can't do that. He can't compromise. Well, my dear, there is just one thing for it. I shall have to tell him the truth myself.'

Emerald gave a mournful little laugh. 'He wouldn't believe you any more than he believes me! He would say, quite rightly, that you cannot possibly know what happened or did not happen between Andrew and me that night . . .'

'That was not what I meant when I said I would tell him the truth,' Saul interrupted quietly. 'I shall tell him that I have known for some time that both Andrew and Claire had lied to me, that they are very much in love, and that Andrew would not touch another woman but my wife.'

Emerald stared at him. 'You—you *knew*? And all the time . . .'

'I pretended. I played my own part in the charade.' He gave her a twisted smile. 'As I've said before, unlike Judah, I'm able to compromise, to settle for what I can get. But I cannot allow your future, and that of your child, to be blighted. I shall tell Judah the truth.'

'Oh, Saul!' Emerald's voice shook. 'How like you to be so generous. But Judah would refuse to believe you. He sees Claire's genuine devotion to you . . .'

'I shall tell him in such a way that he will be forced to believe me,' Saul assured her quietly. He reached for her hand, and held it in his for a moment. 'Leave things to me. Tomorrow, I promise you, Judah will learn the truth.'

She stooped and kissed him, and allowed herself to hope. Saul had sounded so very confident that she could not help being affected by it herself.

Judah did not work late on his accounts as usual that evening. Instead he retired almost immediately after supper, looking obviously exhausted. When Emerald entered their room later she stood for a while, looking down at him by the candle-light as he slept on the sofa, and she thought, *Tonight will be the last time, my darling. And the first thing I'll do, once Saul has convinced you of the truth, is to consign this wretched sofa to one of the spare rooms . . .*

She woke in the morning with a nebulous feeling of something good which was about to happen, and suddenly remembered. She rolled over in bed. Judah was already up, and dressed in his breeches, and was about to pull his shirt over his head.

At that moment someone banged urgently on

their door, and Emerald reached for her wrap. Judah strode to the door and, as he opened it, Claire almost fell into the room, looking wild and distraught.

'I can't waken Saul!' she cried, 'I—I think—I'm not sure . . .'

Judah thrust her to one side and rushed from the room. Her mood changed now to one of impending doom, Emerald followed with Claire in his wake.

Saul lay quite still in bed where the convict servants had placed him the night before, and looked as though he were asleep. Judah touched his face, and then pulled the covers away, placing his ear against his brother's chest.

Judah's face looked gaunt when he straightened. 'He is dead,' he announced starkly. 'He must have died in his sleep.'

'He—he told me—' Claire said through chattering teeth, 'that he—suspected his immobility, his lack of exercise, had affected his heart . . .'

'That is entirely possible,' Judah agreed in a sombre voice.

The two male convicts who had put Saul to bed were called in and questioned, but could shed no light on the matter. Saul had seemed as usual to them the night before, and had not complained of pain or of feeling unwell. He must have suffered a heart seizure during the night.

Claire sobbed uncontrollably, and Judah's eyes were shadowed and haunted as he set about preparing for his brother's funeral.

And even in the midst of her own genuine grief, Emerald could not help remembering that promise which Saul had made to her the evening before his death, and which had inspired her with so much hope.

It was a promise which Fate, with the utmost cruelty of timing, had prevented him from keeping.

CHAPTER ELEVEN

GRIEF HUNG like a pall over the household on the day of the funeral. With people arriving in a steady stream to pay their last respects, Emerald was told by Alice that the two children could not be found.

'I wanted to see that they were properly dressed for the service, madam, but they had disappeared, and I've looked everywhere for them.'

A general search for the children was instigated, but it was Emerald who found them in the end. They were hiding in the corner of the barn behind a bale of hay, holding on to one another and weeping.

Emerald knelt beside them. 'Oh, my darlings, I know how sad you are! We are all of us sad.'

'First—first it was our mother and our father who died,' Timothy sobbed. 'And now Uncle Saul . . . *Everyone dies*. And you don't like us any more . . .'

'I love you,' Emerald interrupted with quiet sincerity. 'And, I promise you, *I* have no intention of dying for a long, long time.'

For some reason this statement caused them to weep even more bitterly, and it was Selina who eventually voiced the major reason for their distress.

'Hettie says—she says Uncle Judah will be sending us to live with Auntie Claire in the new house now—to be her Comfort . . .'

'We don't want to be a Comfort to Auntie Claire!' Timothy cried.

Young as they were, the children sensed the trap which the phrase implied. With Saul dead, they could not contemplate the thought of being made the whole of Claire's world. And of course, they had no inkling of the fact that Andrew was waiting in the wings, ready to fulfil that role.

'You *won't* be going to live with your Auntie Claire,' she promised rashly. 'You're staying here, where I can look after you.' Judah owes me *something*, she thought; he must be made to give way on this.

But when she spoke to him, just before the funeral, he did not oppose her as she had expected. Instead, he said, 'Claire has asked if she may remain here with us from now on, and naturally I have agreed. So the children will stay, too.'

Emerald was puzzled. He had spoken as if it were to be a permanent arrangement that Claire should go on living with them, but surely her passion for Andrew was as strong as her grief for Saul, and she would wish to be with her lover after a respectable period had elapsed?

The funeral itself was an infinitely sad one, and Emerald's heart went out to Judah in particular. Unlike Claire, he was not able to give way to his grief, but bottled it up inside him instead.

The only tangible sign he gave that his brother's death had hit him hard was the way in which he always turned his head when he had to pass the locked door of the room in which Saul had died.

Claire herself had locked the door; after Saul's

body had been removed and the bed had been stripped, she had insisted on everything being left exactly as it was, and had moved into another spare room.

As the weeks passed, Emerald could see all hope for herself and Judah dispersing like mist before the sun. His grief made him even more distant and aloof than before, and Claire did not seek excuses to see Andrew, as Emerald had expected.

Instead, she left it to Judah to communicate with him by letter on matters regarding Saul's station. And in spite of her declared hatred of the colony, she did not mention returning to England. She was the very personification of grieving widowhood.

In desperation, Emerald tackled her one day. 'Saul is dead, and he can't be hurt by anything any more. Won't you tell Judah the truth now, about yourself and Andrew?'

'And strip my husband's memory of all pride?' Claire returned with hostility. 'Oh, no!'

'Saul knew,' Emerald said quietly. 'About you and Andrew, I mean. He told me so on the evening before he died. He promised to tell Judah the truth.'

'I don't believe you,' Claire said flatly.

Emerald tried a different argument. 'Surely your love for Andrew hasn't come to an abrupt end? Surely the two of you must be planning to marry, now that you're free?'

'Yes, we plan to marry,' Claire confirmed coldly. 'But if you tell Judah, or anyone else, I shall deny it.'

Emerald looked at her in desperation. '*When* do you intend to marry Andrew?'

'Not until I have given Saul the full year's mourning to which his memory is entitled. Meanwhile, out of respect for that memory, I intend to live a life of quiet, virtuous widowhood. No one will have cause to point a finger at me.'

And by the time her year of mourning came to an end, Emerald thought with despair, it would be too late. The sterile pattern between Judah and herself would have become set, and neither of them would be able to break out of it.

But in the meantime she was being haunted by the burden of grief that Judah continued to bottle up inside him. She sensed that the locked door to Saul's room, proclaiming it almost to be a shrine, added to his harrowed feelings, and one afternoon she demanded the key from Claire.

'Why?' Claire stalled.

'Alice and I want to clean and air it. Keeping the door locked is morbid and unhealthy. We'll pack Saul's belongings in a trunk, if you can't face the task.'

Reluctantly, Claire handed over the key, and Emerald called Alice to help her. When Judah had to pass the room that evening on his way to bed she wanted the door to be flung wide, showing an ordinary, clean room and not a symbol of his brother's death.

As they went about their tasks, Alice suddenly said, 'You know, madam, that I shall gain my freedom in one month's time.'

'Oh! I was not aware of it, but I am very glad for you, Alice. What will you do? If you wished to stay on here . . .'

Alice shook her head, smiling faintly. 'Thank you, madam, but I am to be married.'

'*Married!*' Emerald stared at her in astonishment. 'To whom? Oh—I beg your pardon—I have no right . . .'

'I don't in the least mind telling you, madam. Do you remember the dragoons who arrived here that day to tell Mr Renshaw that he was to be made a magistrate?'

'Indeed I do! Handsome, impressive-looking fellows they were; both Selina and Timothy were much taken with them.'

Alice's smile made it plain that the children had not been the only ones to be taken by the dragoons—or at any rate by one of them.

'While the convicts were searching for Mr Renshaw,' she went on, 'I fell into conversation with the fair-haired dragoon. His name is Barry Cavendish, and since that day he has been writing to me regularly.' A flush stained her face. 'He—also found a few opportunities for us to meet secretly in the township . . . I tried all I could to discourage him, for his own sake, because he cannot marry an ex-convict and remain a dragoon. But he was quite unshakeable, madam. He has already resigned his post and acquired a free grant of land not far from here, and we are to be married as soon as my period of servitude comes to an end.'

Emerald went and hugged her. 'Oh, Alice, I am so happy for you!' she said sincerely. 'And when you are married, and we are neighbours, I hope we may also be friends, and that you will call me Emerald instead of madam!'

'It would give me the greatest pleasure, madam.' Alice's face glowed with happiness.

The two of them continued to work in the room, and Emerald could not prevent her thoughts from taking a sombre turn. Claire was marking time before she married Andrew, and now Alice, too, was to marry a man whom she obviously loved and who loved her enough in turn to have made sacrifices for her.

Only Emerald herself was doomed to an empty and bleak future . . .

She tried to give all her concentration to what she was doing. While she went through the drawers of the bureau, removing Saul's possessions and storing them in a trunk, Alice was dusting and polishing the floor and the furniture. She was working on the mahogany headboard of the bed when Emerald heard her exclaim, 'There's something caught in here, madam, between the mattress and the headboard. Ah—I've got it.'

She brought out a medicine-bottle wrapped in a sheet of writing-paper, and handed it to Emerald.

The bottle was empty, but it had once contained laudanum. And as Emerald straightened out the paper in which it had been wrapped, and read a sentence or two, a sound escaped her. She looked up.

'Will you go and find Mr Renshaw, please, Alice, and ask him to come at once. And then leave us alone together.'

The housekeeper masked her curiosity well, and hurried from the room. Some minutes later, Judah entered with obvious reluctance, a spasm twisting his face as he looked round the room in which his brother had died.

'I want you to read this, Judah,' Emerald said quietly. 'It was addressed to you.'

She indicated the sheet of paper spread out in front of her on the dressing table, and he came to stand beside her, reading over her shoulder.

Dear Judah,

This evening I made your wife a promise. I gave her my word that by the morning you would know the truth. I am about to honour that promise.

I have known for some weeks now that what was between Andrew and Claire was not merely an affair but a deep and passionate love, and that in spite of the lies they told to spare my feelings, it has never wavered.

I chose to go on pretending that I believed the lies. It made life easier for all three of us, and more important still, it gave Claire the chance of regaining your respect. Because of it, others have stopped ostracising her, and that meant a great deal to her.

You have never understood the relationship between myself and Claire, because you are so different from me, Judah. Claire loves Andrew with passion, but she satisfies her frustrated maternal feelings by caring for me with genuine devotion. I have come to be grateful for what little I can get, but I can see now that I have also come to be selfish.

I have been content to condemn my dearest Claire, whom I love deeply, to a lifetime spent in caring for a helpless cripple who can never give her children, who can never give her physical love. I have been condemning her and Andrew to a life of furtively snatched moments together, a life which will never be fulfilled while I am alive. And I have allowed a lie to be built up which has destroyed your belief in Emerald, and which threatens to wreck both your lives. Andrew is not the father of the child she is expecting, because Emerald loves only you, just as Andrew is totally committed to Claire.

There is only one thing which it is within my power to give all four of you—*freedom*. Physical freedom for Andrew and Claire; freedom from doubts and suspicions between you and Emerald. I give it to you gladly.

You are aware that my taking laudanum to help me sleep has troubled Claire. Well, without telling her—fearful of being tempted to resort to it again, and at the same time wishing it to come as a pleasant surprise to her when I finally announced that I was no longer dependent on the drug—I have refrained from taking any for several weeks now. There is sufficient in the bottle to provide a fatal dose.

I have just swallowed all of it. Soon my helpers will be arriving to lift me into bed for the last time.

What I have done, I have done gladly, out of my deep and enduring devotion to you all. Be happy with Emerald, who loves you. Give my sweet, beautiful Claire your blessing when she announces her decision to marry Andrew.

Goodbye, little brother, and forgive me for the pain I have given all of you in my selfishness.

Saul.

Emerald heard Judah make a sound deep in this throat when he had reached the end of the letter. She rose, wanting to cradle him in her arms as if he were a child. But he stood there as if carved from stone, his eyes blank and unseeing, and she did not have the courage to touch him.

He moved suddenly, jerkily, and stumbled from

the room. She gazed down at the note. Saul must have wrapped it round the empty medicine-bottle, intending to place it underneath his pillow to be found. But he had obviously already been so affected by the drug that it had become wedged, instead, between the mattress and the headboard.

A deep sigh escaped Emerald. She picked up both note and medicine-bottle and went to look for Claire, who was sewing in her bedroom.

Emerald explained briefly how it had been found, and added, 'You, too, had better read it.'

She watched the colour drain completely from Claire's face as she took in the contents of Saul's last note. Her hands were shaking violently as she placed it on the table afterwards. She looked up at Emerald.

'You are to blame for Saul's death,' she said quietly. 'And I shall never forgive you.'

'That isn't fair . . .'

'Isn't it? If you hadn't gone whining to him, forcing a promise from him . . .' Claire's voice broke. She rose, and began to throw clothes into a trunk. 'I cannot stay in this house, in this hateful colony, any longer,' she went on after a while. 'Andrew and I shall go to Sydney and catch the first available vessel to England. As for you, Emerald— I hope you'll be able to live with what you've done!'

A while later Claire set off in the wagonette, driving herself. Emerald watched her leaving, frozen into a state of numbness.

Was she to blame for what Saul had done? Claire certainly believed so. Had that been Judah's reaction, too? Had Saul's death merely widened the chasm between them?

It seemed that it must be so, for he did not return

to the house and no one knew where he was. The hours dragged by; the children were put to bed, and Emerald sat down alone to a supper with which she toyed listlessly.

She retired to their room later, and mechanically prepared for bed. She was sitting in her night-shift in front of the mirror, brushing her hair, when the door opened and Judah entered.

She addressed his reflection in the mirror, without meeting his eyes. 'If you are hungry, I could find something.'

'No. I shared the convicts' rations on one of the runs.'

'I see . . . I did not know where you had gone, or even whether you meant to return.'

'I visited Saul's grave first.' His voice cracked. 'And then I saddled my horse, and just rode without aim or purpose.'

She stood up and faced him. 'I—had no notion, when Saul promised to tell you the truth, what he had in mind. Claire flatly refused to tell you herself, and I knew you wouldn't believe me if *I* tried to tell you. I suppose you blame me for Saul's death.'

'*Oh God, Emerald!*' Judah interrupted hoarsely. 'If we are to apportion blame, then I . . .'

He stopped, and moved blindly towards her and then he was clinging to her, and she could feel the wetness of his cheek against her own.

After a long while he lifted his head and drew her to the bed. He stretched out beside her, holding her close. 'Forgive me,' he whispered.

'There is nothing to forgive.' She touched his face with gentle fingers.

'Emerald,' he said huskily. 'I am a jealous man, and I'm not likely to change. You're beautiful, and

I love you too much to be able to promise never again to suspect you or punish you if you so much as looked at another man.'

'I'm not likely to, my love,' she whispered. 'You are all I want in a man.'

His fingers moved to the fastenings of her nightgown and then he was kissing her exposed breasts with light, feathery touches of his lips which set the blood leaping in her veins. But there was one remaining matter between them which would have to be cleared up before the slate could finally be wiped clean.

She locked her hands gently in his hair, and forced him to meet her eyes.

'Judah—you commented once on my—my un-virgin-like reaction that day when you—when you . . .'

'When I raped you,' he supplied with deep self-loathing.

'Don't look like that!' She rubbed her fingers over the contours of his mouth. 'I want to explain to you. I forced myself not to cry out, because I knew—I sensed—that you had been driven to a point where you needed some violent outlet for all you had been enduring. I made myself submissive, and I even tried to respond because I had realised that I loved you, and I wished to comfort you.'

He closed his eyes in agony. 'Oh, dear God . . . My poor little darling. A virgin—and I raped you—*and you tried to respond* . . .'

'It's over, my love.' She moved her face to seek his lips, and said against his mouth, 'Now teach me—all I need to know—in order to respond properly.'

He proceeded to do just that. His ardour, the

tenderness of his touch and the infinitely loving gentleness with which he brought her to a state of almost unbearable arousal could not have been in sharper contrast to what had happened between them before. And when his body finally claimed hers she found herself soaring to heights of passion which she had never before imagined.

Afterwards she lay, sated with happiness, within the circle of his arms. His hands came up to stroke the damp tendrils of hair away from her face.

'Saul and I were different in many ways,' he said, his voice thick with emotion. 'But in one respect we were alike. When we love, it is completely and for ever.'

She lifted her arms and locked them around his neck, knowing that he had spoken the simple truth.

Your chance to step into the past Take 2 Books FREE

Discover a world long vanished. An age of chivalry and intrigue, powerful desires and exotic locations. Read about true love found by soldiers and statesmen, princesses and serving girls. All written as only Mills & Boon's top-selling authors know how. Become a regular reader of Mills & Boon Masquerade Historical Romances and enjoy 4 superb, new titles every two months, plus a whole range of special benefits: your very own personal membership card entitles you to a regular free newsletter packed with recipes, competitions, exclusive book offers plus other bargain offers and big cash savings.

AND an Introductory FREE GIFT for YOU.
Turn over the page for details.

Fill in and send this coupon back today and we will send you

2 Introductory Historical Romances FREE

At the same time we will reserve a subscription to Mills & Boon Masquerade Historical Romances for you. Every two months you will receive Four new, superb titles delivered direct to your door. You don't pay extra for delivery. Postage and packing is always completely free. There is no obligation or commitment – you only receive books for as long as you want to.

Just fill in and post the coupon today to MILLS & BOON READER SERVICE, FREEPOST, P.O. BOX 236, CROYDON, SURREY CR9 9EL.

Please Note:- READERS IN SOUTH AFRICA write to Mills & Boon, Postbag X3010, Randburg 2125, S. Africa.

FREE BOOKS CERTIFICATE

To: Mills & Boon Reader Service, FREEPOST, P.O. Box 236, Croydon, Surrey CR9 9EL.

Please send me, free and without obligation, two Masquerade Historical Romances, and reserve a Reader Service Subscription for me. If I decide to subscribe I shall receive, following my free parcel of books, four new Masquerade Historical Romances every two months for £5.00, post and packing free. If I decide not to subscribe, I shall write to you within 10 days. The free books are mine to keep in any case. I understand that I may cancel my subscription at any time simply by writing to you. I am over 18 years of age.

Please write in BLOCK CAPITALS.

Signature _____

Name _____

Address _____

_____ Post code _____

SEND NO MONEY — TAKE NO RISKS.

Please don't forget to include your Postcode.

Remember, postcodes speed delivery. Offer applies in UK only and is not valid to present subscribers. Mills & Boon reserve the right to exercise discretion in granting membership. If price changes are necessary you will be notified.

4M Offer expires December 24th 1984.

EP9M